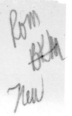

ROMANCE

Large Print Har
Hart, Francis, 1916-
Love is a secret

et

G·K
Hall
&Cº.

Love is a Secret

Francis Hart

G.K. Hall & Co. • Thorndike, Maine

Published in 2000 by arrangement with Golden West Literary Agency.

G.K. Hall Large Print Paperback Series.

The text of this Large Print edition is unabridged.
Other aspects of the book may vary from the original edition.

Set in 16 pt. Plantin by Al Chase.

Printed in the United States on permanent paper.

ISBN 0-7838-8794-9

CONTENTS

CHAPTER ONE

Circa *Now*

One got the feeling as though it were a Venezuelan jungle or an African rain forest. One extreme case had described it as strolling at the bottom of the sea.

The world was a varying degree of green from extremely dark to palest, pale green, with this prismatic high haziness that diffused everything shattering sunbeams and scattering dull gold.

And soundless. Although there seemed a gently heaving roll at this sea-bottom place, one could never detect a sound. Never. It was incredible that sometime, something wouldn't make a sound. It was the only genuine place on earth where there never had been and never was a single sound of any kind.

But there was a compensatory factor; there was always movement. The entire undersea universe rolled and settled and rolled again. Not really. One only had that unearthly sensation. Two things could come together and soundlessly keep cadence to that unseen, unheard, undersea tug and tow.

Well; that's how one person had described it. 'Not,' he'd said, 'so much a place, as a sensation. You know; like heaven and hell. But real enough the same way the fourth dimension is real.'

It was real enough. No one had ever stubbed his toe against heaven or hell. At least no one had ever related such an occurrence. But here that was very possible.

As for the sensation, yes of course, but then people had all manner of sensations. An individual is not simply a gobbet of lymph and tissues endowed with ambulatory propensities. He has also antennae of a highly sensitive complex of invisible coloured emanations which stretch in all directions, sometimes for hundreds of feet, sometimes for miles. Radar-like, everything his probes contact flash back to his flesh — substance, his antennae, creating some variety of sensation.

But abstractions didn't apply, factual though they might have been. Nor did the sea-floor feeling entirely satisfy. An environment could, very often did, affect individuals two ways — through sense and sight — but a hand upon stone, eyes facing an unrelenting greeny endlessness, or feet treading earthen paths, had to acknowledge that which was felt, seen, stood upon, for in *this* dimension at least the world is bruisingly hard and real.

Eric had once drawn a sketch in summer dust outlining all the boundaries, confessing however that southward no one really knew, they could only surmise. But in every other direction explorations had definitely fixed what lay beyond. And of course they *did* know what lay southward too, but it was a thing they closed their minds against. Their greenery world was a belted bulwark between them, their village, and the south-ward lands. More than a hundred miles of emerald-dark green. Trees that stood stiffly towards the heavens, thick as grain in the fields, silent as death and nearly as gloomy in the cool shadowy places.

Einer, before he had died in the depths of winter, had called it their 'forest of fear'. It was perhaps the best of all descriptions. Like the foetid jungle it had natural pitfalls. Also like Venezuela or Africa, it had silent shadows that shot without warning.

This 'little war' as Eric called it, had been in progress for a very long while. But there were rules. The stalkers fought in utter silence; they never moved out into the clearings where villages and towns lay, they never annoyed traffic on the paved roads, they did not kill indiscriminately.

Helene's father had once snorted disdain for what others called gallantry. 'They are nothing but murderers,' he'd said. 'Filthy assassins. The reason they don't attack towns is because there aren't enough of them left. The reason they daren't interfere on the roads is because that would bring the soldiers to wipe them out. They are nothing but *Germans!*'

He'd used that designation as though to imply they were less than humans; meaning they were on a level with marauding wolves or other animals. He wasn't alone in this feeling. There is no such thing as an heroic, vanquished conqueror. When *Festung Europa* dissolved in flame, bands of the Supermen lingered as brigands.

'It is incredible,' Helene's father said to the village mayor, Gunnar Mainpaa. 'Look at those supersonic aircraft in the sky. Consider the immense lorries, the wireless in almost every house bringing voices into our homes from every corner of the world. And yet these people slip about like Red Indians. We live with one foot in the twentieth century, the other foot in the sixteenth century.'

Old Gunnar had smiled. 'That is exactly how we live, Franz. Some of the people live in hide houses and drive reindeer here and there, unchanged for a thousand years. Others have their wireless, their automobiles, even fly away in aeroplanes. It shouldn't be so astonishing to you that through the southward forests men still stalk one another. My old friend, consider: the machines march ahead very swiftly, but *we* — well — it takes us ten thousand years just to add one speck of pigment to our skins.'

Franz told Marta that same evening Gunnar Mainpaa was getting so old he was philosophical about everything, and while that doubtless was a virtue among old people, it certainly was an unrealistic attitude to take towards this infernal, ceaseless butchery.

Marta could easily agree for she'd only just returned home from Eisens where young Gust still lay in a coma from the bullet in his head. In her opinion, like the view of her husband, there was nothing on earth as thoroughly despicable as a

German. She had survived the Occupation twenty and more years earlier with that indelible hatred firmly fixed, part of her heart, part of her psyche.

'It's the government,' she said bitterly, working at the stove. 'What do people care who live in places like Helsinki, so far from here? I heard that census-taker say it was up to the local constabulary to take care of bandits and when Trygve said how could local people be expected to bunt those men down through a forest that stretched across three provinces, the census-taker only suggested co-operation among the provincial police. He didn't care. He had no idea what is going on. It is the government. . . . Probably it is friendly with the Germans now and doesn't want to mention anything that could make an awkward situation.'

Franz poured coffee and drank it scalding hot and black. 'I know. Last year when Einer was alive a man came to the store saying there was some of this kind of thing going on everywhere; all we had to do was be patient; the Germans would get too old, or would be converted to peaceful ways, or would settle down, take land and marry.'

'He should see young Eisen,' muttered Marta. She remembered something and looked at her husband. 'Where is Helene?'

Taking up a cloth to dry his coarse moustache so the coffee wouldn't stain it, he said, 'Upstairs. I brought her home with me from the store.'

11

Evidently that was a satisfactory reply for Marta moved her thick, sturdy body between stove and table, drainboard and cupboards saying nothing more. But her face still wore the expression of a mother who'd seen the anguish in the home of other parents; a bleak and tortured look, part anguish, part fierce resentment.

Her husband was also thick and sturdy, although running now to paunch, thin hair and heavy jowls. His eyes had the faint hint of an upward slant which was common among the people. The face was flat and round, but strong and hardy. Some of the people were more Mongoloid. Dead Einer for instance had been teased in his youth because he'd looked almost Chinese or Mongolian. And of course there were the Laplanders who not only looked and acted Mongolian but even lived as those ancient scourges of the top of the world had lived.

The foreign teacher they'd had three years previously at the school had once traced out the gradual steps of the ethnic groups starting back with the Mongolians, then moving down the map from top to bottom to show how the historic pure-bloods had imprinted their stamp in the far north, while those who roamed southward met tribesmen pushing northward from Teutonic lands. In the course of many centuries, many forays and wars and peaceful interminglings, a blending had occurred which altered the people, except in the far north, until they were a fusion of different tribes.

Then, or so said this outlander, had evolved the nation-states, the boundaries, the delineating lines which stated all below were Germans — Austrians, Prussians, Bavarians — but still Germans, while all above were Finns, Norwegians, Swedes, Danes. And then, said the alien, the real troubles had come. Immense wars, economic squeezes, national instead of ethnic friction, disputes over such free things as waterways, woodlands, ore-bearing mountain chains, grass tundras, fishing rights, grazing rights. Even the right of one or the other to fly through the free air above.

The teacher had been expelled. Everyone understood perfectly; when one lived side by side with the Russian Bear one did not show much wisdom by taking into one's village the cub.

Still, now and then in guarded tones the villagers recalled his words. 'Asinine,' he'd called an alleged violation of Finnish air-sovereignty. 'No one owns the air. It is to breathe, to savour, to enjoy. Finland doesn't own it. Neither Germany nor Russia own the air. It is everywhere; belongs to everyone. The same with the sea.'

Gunnar Mainpaa said the man was a dangerous communist. Franz'd had doubts of that but he was also a businessman. When one dealt with the public and was dependent upon its goodwill as well as its cash, one did not fly in the face of the popular will. Still, as he once said to his daughter at lunch in the backroom of the store, 'If the man had been a communist, why did he say the air didn't belong to Russia; why did he always insist the world was for *all* men to exploit and enjoy, instead of just some men? No; I don't think he's a communist. But I certainly don't know what he is.'

It didn't matter; the week following Mayor Mainpaa's denunciation the instructor was called away and never returned. But then that didn't matter either. There were always plenty of instructors for the school. Some of these were suspect, but they were much more subtle than the alien had been. They knew ways to reach young minds without once raising uneasiness. They were real professionals where the alien had been simply a freethinker.

Well; people always learn to live with crises. The longer they teeter upon the razor's edge the more adept they become, and because inherently no one wishes to disrupt orderliness, peaceful existence, commercial sequences, the more they vilify those who would warn of impending danger — even though they know perfectly well that danger is close.

But when a neighbour's son lies near death with a bullet inside his skull, that makes a lot of difference. Only then people don't want to do much themselves, they want their government to do it. Or, as Franz said at supper that night, 'Why do we pay taxes anyway — ruinous ones at that — if not to be protected; the government is going to *have* to do something about those filthy Germans.'

CHAPTER TWO

A Time For A Mother's Tears

The village of Joki was beside a river with the same name and while the Gulf of Bothnia was not far distant the people of the village of Joki received whatever waterway trade and sustenance they required from the River Joki.

There was an immense estuary with many bristling little islands, dark places of trees and underbrush in the hot, sudden summers, places of grotesque shapes and whiteness in the long, dark winters.

Joki had no industry but its commerce was bustling and thriving. Franz Vasaanen's store in its stout log building did a good business among fishermen, woodsmen, farmers, artisans. Gunnar Mainpaa's shop, dealing in clothing of all kinds, held in disdain by village people but highly prized by country people, was next to the Vasaanen building, so even if the two men hadn't already been friends it was probable propinquity would have made them so.

Helene Vasaanen — named for the English nurse who had delivered her in a terrible storm eighteen winters before — often referred to Gunnar, the half-Swede, as 'uncle', although there was no actual relationship.

Joki was by Finnish standards a cosmopolitan

village. Lying near Sweden its language as well as its customs had much of both nationalities, and oddly enough, while Germans were despised by the older generation with an ardour equal to the rancour their fathers had evinced towards the Russians, the actual fact was that those brigands haunting the forests were not entirely Germanic.

In fact a pompous army officer who'd made an investigation two years earlier — the summer after that foreign schoolmaster had been whisked away — said that the brigands were Balts, Russians — mostly Russians — with only a few Germans in the bands, And Swedes.

Still, to Franz Vasaanen and Gunnar Mainpaa and Trygve Vesainen, the Eisens, and Eric Vendson who knew most because, as a professional hunter he'd led most of the hunting parties, they were Germans. But then, as Helene once ventured to say in her mother's presence, *German* didn't mean *people;* it meant something very bad, something despicable. Like calling someone a vile name.

Marta hadn't disputed that but she'd said, 'You were born too late to know what beasts they are; what butchers and devils. A German is the worst kind of man.'

Helene *had* been born too late, but as old Einer might have said had he lived, there is a wedge driven between the generations the moment a baby arrives; that wedge goes deeper, spreads wider, each year until at eighteen the generations scarcely speak the same language and most certainly do not think the same thoughts.

Helene knew a German; a student cycling through Scandinavia with other students. His name was Hans. He was tall, very fair and very handsome. He laughed easily, had talented hands and was interested in the customs and traditions of Finland.

She met him at a hostel on the southerly outskirts of Joki and he'd lingered a few days after his friends had gone on to stroll in the forest with her, sit by the river, or eat a little lunch with her in the shade of the spruces down where the Joki road twisted and turned towards its juncture with a great throughway leading to the industrial community of Raanujarvï.

She had reason enough for never mentioning Hans, but after all Joki was a small, insular place. It had been correctly stated that if one shouted in the centre of the village on the outskirts everyone could immediately say who had cried out, and even why they had done so.

They never talked of the war, which was over before either had been born and really wasn't part of their world anyway. Hans talked of his schooling — he was to be an engineer in another two years, fully qualified and employable if, as he laughed, anyone was interested in hiring a fully qualified but woefully inexperienced engineer.

Then he had to go on.

Helene didn't weep; she didn't come of weeping stock. But she went listlessly to the places where they'd been and sat and held her arms about both knees listening to the silent echo of his musical laughter, thinking of the softness of his lips, the gentleness of his hands, the tumbling fairness of his curly hair.

It was like a dagger being twisted when Gust Eisen died because then again all the old rancour came to life; a German brigand had shot Gust in the head. Those filthy Huns were killing honest, decent people for no reason except that Huns only killed and destroyed. Read it in the history books or better yet, ask men like Eric Vendson the big, grim Swede who lived alone in a log house on the outskirts and whose entire mature lifetime had been spent killing Germans, first in Sweden, then in the Underground during the war, and now, nearly thirty years later, in the forests of Finland.

Ask Trygve Vesainen whose parents had starved to death in the snow while being whipped along on their way to slave camps during the war. Or any of the people who'd lost brothers or friends or even sons and daughters.

The history books told a clean, analytical story but life-experience walking the roadways of Joki told another story altogether. Helene's father said the Russians, bad as they were, at least were a kindred people. Oh; their communism was no good, but it was only a phase. The Russians were always going through phases.

18

Indeed, they killed Finns too, but not as the Germans had done and were still doing. If Franz had his way the troops would build blockhouses through the forest and exterminate those two-legged Hun vermin.

Hate runs deep, Helene knew. She also learned in her eighteenth year it is stronger than love — among the older people, but then their juices were drying, their purpose for being had already been expiated. They'd had their children, reared the families, suffered their personal losses and privations. All that was left to fill their days was work and memory — and hatred.

She grew moody as the days ran along after Hans left. Sometimes at the store she sat at the books looking at nothing. Her father, after speaking to her twice without a flicker of reciprocity, once asked if she were ill. After that she was a little more alert, but it was a difficult month and in fact her father said something to that effect to her mother.

'Maybe she should leave the village; go down to one of the cities for schooling, or perhaps just go somewhere for a few weeks.'

Marta was brusque. 'Where? And what's the use? It's the heat.'

It could have been at that. Finns suffered more during their brief, hot summers than they ever did from their long cold winters. They wilted when the heat got above eighty degrees Fahrenheit.

The log store did not have a very high roof

except right at the peak where it was very steep in order to shed snow. Still, since the walls were massively thick, it usually was several degrees cooler inside than outside. Other people, including girls Helene's age, didn't seem to suffer too much. In fact Helene herself hadn't suffered noticeably in former summers.

'Well,' said Franz Vasaanen crossly to Marta one morning after Helene had gone ahead to open the store, 'whatever it is must end soon. The mistakes in the books are considerable. I can't put up with it much longer, my own daughter or not.'

They had buried the Eisen youth, a good deal of the anger, indignation and sadness had atrophied, and the summer ran on. Eric said he'd located a cold camp where Germans had stayed, not three miles from Joki. Gunnar was patient about that.

'With Eric it is an obsession. You've got to make allowances. I think for him the war has never ended. He can't work on the boats or in the mills. He can't even live close to others. Something stopped inside him a quarter of a century ago over in Sweden so he came here, maybe because we're more isolated, maybe because we have the forests — and the other men with guns. I can't properly explain what it is I feel with Eric, but still, I feel it, and I'm prompted to say we mustn't let him rush us into anything.'

Helene's listlessness didn't increase, particularly, but it became more noticeable to her parents. She was a beautiful girl. Tall, which was uncommon among Finns, especially among Finnish women, very fair and strong and now, suntanned to the texture of cream. She always had an escort when there was a party, a dance, or a group went to the cinema at one of the larger towns some miles distant. Or boating; she was a superb swimmer. Boys always came back again and again.

That was what became more noticeable; she didn't want to go with the others her age. She'd sit at home or perhaps go walking off by herself in the evenings, never saying very much.

'She's meeting someone,' her father said.

Marta knew otherwise. 'A girl doesn't go to meet even another girl wearing a face like that. If it were a boy she'd be alive, her eyes would sparkle.' Marta looked at her husband. It was disconcerting — in fact it was annoying — how soon men forgot.

'Then what is it for God's sake?' he exploded. 'Marta, talk to her. I'm at the end of my tether. Either she acts normal again or . . .'

'Or what, Franz?'

'Or I don't know, Marta. I'm at a loss. What can it be; she's not in love, she's not ill, she's not restless or bored or, or . . . just talk to her.'

Marta was of the solid folk. She rushed at nothing nor did she push anything, least of all the daughter who was the apple of her eye, the song of her heart, the dream of her mind.

She had no idea what was troubling Helene or even if anything really was troubling her. She only knew Helene hadn't been acting the same for a month or more now.

God!

She sank down at the breakfast table, her heart making a queer, tingly thrust in her bosom. But no, it was a terrible thought; it was a vile thing to suspect one's own daughter of.

Still, the time element was about right. On the other hand it was also right for other things as well.

Marta sat like stone feeling herself age. She had a strong continuum of energy. Now it deserted her, left her sitting on the chair as though she were a hundred years of age and weighed as many stone; too old and heavy to even stand upright.

She was like that a long while but the urge to do a particular thing nagged, so eventually she went upstairs under the eaves to her daughter's room and rummaged. After all two women living close in the same house shared secrets voluntarily or inadvertently.

The truth came a half hour later. The evidence was obvious. She stumbled back down to the parlour and fell into a chair with a blackness all round, with a difficulty besetting her even at such a simple thing as breathing.

Some women might cry, some might hurl themselves about, some might rush away to talk, feeling the age-old female compulsion stronger than ever at this moment. But Marta Vasaanen simply sat and looked out where hot summer sunlight peeled away shadows layer by layer as the morning advanced.

Franz. . . . What would Franz do?

A woman lived with a man so many, many years, and always he did something unexpected. She had no idea about Franz's reaction beyond thinking there definitely would be one.

She wanted to weep and couldn't even do that. Her eyes were so dry they grated in their sockets. She was cold despite sweaty palms.

Her beautiful daughter was pregnant! The child she'd always known would marry very well, perhaps a wealthy man from the large cities, at the very least some handsome, dashing American or English tourist, perhaps, was now with child and without husband.

Of course Helene had been different this past month. Why shouldn't she be different; every day that passed without the event would make her more and more different; more troubled and upset, more lackadaisical and alone.

At noon Marta went to the kitchen for tea and didn't do more than boil the water before she forgot all about tea and went out back where the flowers flourished carrying that burden she could scarcely move under.

Of course one had to be practical. Whether one's heart was crushed and bleeding or not, one had to be practical. How many times had Franz said that: being practical minimizes the risk.

All right. Marta would be practical. Then who was the man; and it didn't matter any longer what his position, it only mattered that he married Helene.

Franz would see that — after the grief and shock. Franz would find the young man and see that whatever could be salvaged for his daughter was saved.

Finally, Marta could cry. Six hours after the full import had hit her making her reel to a chair, she could cry. And she did, hunched over rocking back and forth with deep-down racking spasms tearing her apart inside.

CHAPTER THREE

The Feelings Of Women

Helene returned early from the store with the information that her father'd had an opportunity to go to Raanujarvï with Gunnar and Trygve Vesainen, who owned an automobile. He asked his daughter to tell Marta he would be back within two days. Helene faintly smiled as she said, 'Trygve needed some steel for a boat, Gunnar had to get some bolts of cloth, and father — well — father said a little lamely he'd try and pick up some of the things we are short of at the store.'

Marta shrugged and bent over the oven. She didn't look at her daughter right away. Of course it had been eight or nine hours since she'd come to her conclusion so a good deal of the shock was gone, but the agony was no less, nor was the worry and sensation of sickness.

Helene went to bathe and get into the loose housedress she normally wore at home. Her mother set only two places at the table. When Helene returned she motioned for her to be seated then, gripping a cup across the table she said, 'I know what it is to be young, Helene. I also know what it's like to love a man very much.' She remembered something and also said, 'Men forget. Well; everyone has a function. Perhaps men should forget; once they have a wife things change. They must then work and plan. Normally, your father and I would have had several children. But we were already getting along in years as it was. The war did that; it disrupted lives as though individuals weren't important.'

Helene's lovely eyes grew very still as her mother rambled on. She guessed, long before Marta got to the kernel of the subject. There was no doubt of that because her face turned very white, her eyes got dry and staring.

'But now there is no war,' Marta was saying. 'Those Germans in the forest, yes, but no war that levels whole villages and leaves people to die in the snow, freeze in holes they've dug in the sod. So now women can plan better.'

Marta stopped for breath. For a moment or two the sound of her own voice had been comforting. Now it no longer was. Now it sounded garrulous and cranky — and cowardly. She knew what she had to say, and couldn't say it.

Helene helped her. 'Mother; I'm sorry. It wasn't supposed to hurt you too.'

'Hurt me,' said Marta dully, stripped down at last to what lay between them. 'Hurt me . . .' Marta sniffled.

Helene burst into tears, threw herself out of the chair, flung round and fled.

Marta's grip on the cup loosened. She lifted the thing and sipped. The brew was hot, which was pleasant, and it was acidy, which was real. She pushed back at the table and became very calm and thoughtful. A person who has lived through so much should know something. After all, Helene was not the first nor would she be the last, and the entire sequence followed natural laws.

But she had very few answers. The ones she had were not good answers. The shame — well — barring a miracle she and Franz must now accept the inevitability of the shame, for their village was a small place, few had secrets and nothing as obvious as a big belly could remain a secret for very long.

They could send her away, which would fool their neighbours undoubtedly, but what did they say when their girl returned with her squirming bundle?

She finished the coffee, automatically cleaned up her kitchen and thought she wasn't looking at the thing properly at all. What *really* mattered was her child. She dried both hands, hung up the apron and went sturdily across the parlour, up the stairs and into her daughter's room.

Helene was no longer weeping. She was sitting in front of the window looking out, dry-eyed and white as death.

Marta patted her shoulder standing behind the chair. 'Does he want to marry you?' she asked softly. 'Is it wise to let this go on so long?'

Helene raised a cold hand for her mother to take and hold. 'He doesn't know, Mother.'

Marta was surprised. 'Doesn't know? Well, of course you'll have to tell him.'

'I can't. He's gone.'

Marta released the cold hand, moved round to a little straight-backed chair where she could sit and see her daughter's face. 'Gone? What do you mean he is gone? Does that signify that he knew — and ran away?'

'Mother; do you recall some young people passing through a month and a half ago, bicycling on a tour?'

Marta said, 'I remember,' then her face fell inward. 'Germans,' she whispered. 'They were German students.'

Helene sat without moving watching the pain sear up from deep down inside Marta as though her mother had been seized by some deadly illness. The hands in Helene's lap lay like dead birds.

Marta's reflexes were slower than usual. She'd survived a disillusioning day as it was, now this had come to shatter what little strength was left. Helene spoke softly to her.

'He was kind and gentle, Mother. He liked Joki and the people. He was so handsome, so understanding and so well educated.'

'He was a German, Helene.'

'Yes. We didn't talk of the war. He was born after it ended the same as I was.'

Marta made a very valiant effort to rally, and partially succeeded. 'Is he coming back? Where does he live, Helene; he must be told. Even a German may have some decency — although he will be an exception if this is so.'

'He lives in Essen. His name is Hans Einhorst. The group he is with is going through Sweden, then Norway, then back down —'

'Helene, what will your father do? Ahhhh; why must it have been a German?'

Helene said nothing for a long while and meantime the shadows grew and thickened outside where window lights were visible throughout the village and the northern sky turned royal blue with ermine droplets of diamond-brightness. There was a little wind blowing, high above, with tendrils now and then brushing rooftops to create a moaning sound. It was one of those nights, depending upon the moods of people, which was either gentle and lovely, or sad and anguished.

Marta rallied, finally. 'You must come back downstairs,' she said, being practical. 'You must eat some supper.'

'I'm not hungry. I couldn't eat now, Mother.'

'Helene — a *German!*'

Exasperation passed as a soft shadow over the girl's beautiful features then was gone leaving just the patient look, the sad and unhappy look.

'It wasn't meant to happen like this, Mother, but I loved him and he loved me, so I'm not ashamed.'

'Wait,' said her mother a trifle grimly. 'Wait until you can no longer button a dress or use a belt.'

'It was so beautiful, so perfect. He came as though I'd always known he would come; as though I'd been waiting nineteen years, Mother.'

'Eighteen,' corrected her mother. 'I don't know. If Eric knew he would hunt him down and kill him. I just don't know, Helene, what your father will do.'

'Nothing at all,' said the girl, looking directly at Marta. 'It's not his affair.'

Marta was shocked out of her thraldom. 'Not his affair! What kind of a thing is that to say? You are your father's heart and soul. Not his affair! It could kill him. Even if you'd married this — this *German* — it could still kill him. Helene, how can you say such a terrible thing?'

The girl leaned, closed a cold hand over her mother's work-roughened, strong sinewy hand, looked directly into the older woman's eyes and the situation was reversed. She said, 'This is my child, Mother. I'll go away to have it. I'll see that no shame comes to you and father. But I *want* the little boy. At first — no — but I was afraid then. I panicked. Now I've had a month to think. He is mine and I want him — very much.'

Marta slid her hand from beneath the hold of the other, smoother, colder hand. She straightened on the chair. She could understand part of what the girl had said because she'd had powerful instincts years ago when she'd been carrying her own child. But she couldn't understand something else at all.

'Do your parents mean so little to you; don't you realize everyone will find out, sooner or later? No matter if you go away and have the child — and why do you keep saying "him"? — someday you will return to the town with — it. The shame will come back with you. The disgrace.'

'Then I won't ever return, Mother.' The girl's voice was hard and tough with a ring to it. 'There is plenty of work in the big cities. Even down in Helsinki.'

Marta slumped. The dilemma was overpowering. There was no solution. What would Franz say to all this; what must be done? Find the German and bring him back? It was, in Marta's view, a questionable thing. Should Helene have her fatherless child without the German ever knowing, or should she marry a — German? It was a choice no mother should ever have to make who had her own scars, deep-etched, from knowledge of Huns.

She said again Helene must eat and this time the girl dutifully nodded and arose. Marta led the way.

But when they reached the kitchen all they had was coffee.

Helene said, 'Let me tell father.'

Marta was non-committal. *She* didn't want to have to tell him but on the other hand she had no idea what Franz would do. She compromised by saying nothing must be said until they were all at home together.

Franz was not a violent man; Marta had known him back when, as a sturdy stripling, he'd had cause to be violent. He'd acquitted himself well enough, but she'd known then he'd inwardly winced from the things that were done. But again, one never knew.

Helene brought her wandering thoughts back. 'I'm so sorry, Mother.' The girl looked tired and despairing, the strength was gone from her voice as well as from her face. Like most people, she felt more than she could express. Obviously, she'd lived with her problem just long enough by now to realize how grave it really was. But too, she'd filtered a lot of alternatives through her consciousness in a month, by night as well as by day, so she'd faced everything her mother was just now clumsily trying to sort out and grapple with.

Marta never once considered the fact of love after first being told by her daughter that it had been love which had brought all this about. Instead, she tried to devise means for shielding her child while at the same time shielding Franz's name and honour. Within a few days she would realize that one or the other had to take precedent; that there just was no way to assure both.

The pair of silent women went to the parlour and awkwardly sat. Marta said, 'You should have been a boy,' without sounding especially bitter about it.

Helene's reply was quietly spoken. 'Then I'd be on the other side, tonight, wouldn't I? Mother; I know you can't forgive me. I also know I should be more contrite. But except for what people will say, I'm glad because I loved him so terribly much.'

Marta had some knitting. She became busy with it. Normally she reserved knitting for the very long winter nights. Now, she had to have something to occupy her hands, her eyes, to a lesser extent her mind.

Well; young girls get ripe. That was no secret. Young men get swollen necks like the stag reindeers. It is all in the natural pattern of things, except that civilized people have established rules governing such behavior. Marta sighed. That foreign instructor they'd had at the school a few years back would have been able to refine everything to proper perspective — only his explanations couldn't change anything. They might offer solace, but there was still the village, the rules, the disgrace of abrogation. Marta dropped the knitting to her lap. What was the solution, and when they finally had to find it, what good would it do; the damage was done, the scar seared into brain and heart, the anguish felt. None of them would ever forget. She looked at her beautiful, tall and tan daughter with a sting of dry tears, and said, 'It all keeps going round and round. A German, and now this, and whatever's to be done, and the fact that something must be done, and your father. Then — it all starts going round again. Helene . . . ?'

The lovely girl went and knelt beside her mother. They held hands with Marta furiously blinking back the tears.

'Just let Hans be a man,' whispered the girl. 'Please mother, just let him be a *man*. Not a German, just another man. He is so — beautiful, so sweet and gentle.'

Marta couldn't control the tears and when they gushed her daughter locked them both in strong, supple arms so that they could weep together. It was a mingling of tears from two separate eras in time.

CHAPTER FOUR

A Night To Remember

Franz Vasaanen returned on Thursday with a little present for each of them and several packages of things for the store. They gave him all that day to recover from his adventure. They might have permitted him another day as well but he noticed they were different and asked questions. They told him that night after supper when he was lighting an American cigarette in the parlour and he sat like a man who has just been struck very hard; stunned. Shocked into temporary immobility with even his breathing minimal while his eyes looked at them across the room trying to accept, to comprehend.

Finally he said, 'Helene — who?'

This of course was the part Marta hated most. Helene gave her answer slowly and quietly. Each word fell like a steel ball striking glass.

'A boy who came through a month ago with a bicycling group touring the country.'

'A — stranger, Helene, a man you didn't even know?'

'Father, I knew him. He was exactly the man I've always imagined. In every way.'

'Bicycling through. . . .' Franz's eyes shifted a little and fell on Marta. 'You didn't know?'

'Until night before last, Franz.'

'Well then, Marta, do you know who those students were?'

His wife nodded. She knew. She knew all right and she'd lived with the gall of it for two days now. Almost three days in fact.

'Germans, Franz.'

'Ahhhh,' he sighed, looked at the smoking cigarette and slowly broke it in an ashtray grinding it pitilessly until the thing was ruptured and ugly and completely dead.

'Yes, I remember. They came into the store.' Marta listened, watching him closely. It occurred to her he might have seen this particular German. He had. 'It was the tall, nice-looking boy; the one with the smile, was it not?' Marta's eyes flicked sidewards as Helene nodded. 'I remember,' said her father, without adding that when he'd seen that German gaze at his daughter his insides had ground into a painful knot. 'I remember. Helene; I will find him. I'll take Eric and find him.'

Marta spoke swiftly, 'Franz; if you do that it will be much worse.'

'What can be worse!'

'Franz; don't be blinded like I was, at first. Our first consideration is our own child.'

He fumbled at a pocket, brought forth a packet of American cigarettes, evidently purchased down in Raanujarvï as a luxury since such things were exorbitantly expensive, lit one, exhaled the smoke and ran a hand across his coarse moustache looking at neither of them but at the dead, blackened old stone fireplace with dead eyes.

Marta sat back slightly. The first shock had hit him and passed along. Now would come all the frightful thoughts, the dagger-sharp pain plunging deep into one's belly and heart and mind, all at the same time. She knew because she'd been through it hour by hour, day by day, even minute by minute.

She said, 'You always say — be practical. By tomorrow you'll have searched through all the things I've searched through.'

'Father,' murmured Helene, 'it's my child. I want it very much.'

Franz shifted position slightly and gestured with the cigarette. 'Go,' he said. 'Go to bed. Go upstairs.' His voice was thick, not with anger but with a drunken kind of leaden dullness as though his tongue weren't functioning properly. 'Go upstairs, Helene.'

That had been her punishment as a small child, being sent to her room while her parents were sitting in the night with a jolly fire.

She shook her head. 'No.'

Marta intervened. 'You go, Helene,' she murmured, and reached to pat her daughter's hand. 'Please now.'

Helene went.

Franz smoked and seemed to thicken and grow smaller in the chair. Marta saw him age as she herself had aged. He murmured, 'Great God, Marta,' sounding as though he were strangling. 'We sacrificed so much — for this?'

'Well; she says he is a man, Franz.'

'Yes of course he is a man. Damned German stallion; I'll go see Eric in the morning.'

'No you won't. Listen Franz; we have to protect our own.'

'Good God, I thought that's what we did when he educated her, when he explained about — those things — to her.' He lifted darkening, feverish eyes. 'What now of the *real* man she should have married; what now comes of everything? Marta, I don't feel very good tonight.' He said a very earthy Russian word.

They sat for a while in the quiet with night all around. She had to give him the time she'd already had, to get used to this — she tried to find a word in her mind — tragedy sounded too trite, disgrace too remote, trouble too minimal — this disaster. And still she had no idea what his ultimate reaction would be.

'Franz; the boy doesn't know. She doesn't want him to know.'

He blew smoke and dropped his chin to his breast. 'Even if he did know; what of it? He won't ever return and you know that, Marta. Do you recall what the Germans thought of Finns; well, they still think that. Helene was — there. She was willing. It makes me sick to my stomach. She was willing — with a German!'

'She says to think of him as a man; only as a man.'

He looked witheringly at her. 'It had to be a

man. What a foolish thing for you to tell me. Eric is the answer.'

'You know that isn't so, Franz. What good is the boy dead?'

'Well; what good is he alive, tell me?'

'It would be on Helene's conscience. Franz we've got to put everything else aside and think of her.'

He started to say, 'Like she thought of us?' but didn't finish it; instead, put the cigarette back between his lips and deeply dragged on it. Of course Marta was right. 'But she doesn't act ashamed,' he complained. 'Marta; where are the tears?'

'Ahhh; they were there, Franz. There are few left in her now. She shouldn't be up there alone either. Let me go get her.'

'No. No; it should be as it is right now. Marta, I don't know what to do — exactly.'

His wife could understand that readily enough. Now, everything was going round and round for him. 'Go to bed, lie and think and eventually fall asleep. In the morning kiss her cheek at the breakfast table, Franz. That's what I've been doing. She is all we have, really. She didn't think of hurting us. She was a girl in love for the first time.'

'My God what kind of a love was that, Marta?'

'That same kind everyone knows sometimes, Franz, only with her it worked out differently.' Marta arose. 'I'll get some coffee.'

He smoked and didn't raise his eyes until

she'd disappeared, then he glanced sorrowfully at the stairway up which his daughter had walked and run and skipped since childhood. The weight bore him down in his chair with physical force. He had to put out the cigarette; they had tasted very good, now they were flat and vinegary and poisonous.

Marta came back with the cups. He accepted his with a nod and a look. His wife looked the same in the shadowy room but she moved slower, seemed heavier, sat with more finality, as though she did not mean to ever again arise from that chair.

She watched him constantly and that was annoying too; as though she was afraid of what he might do, which was pointless for right at that moment he couldn't even have got out of the chair without help.

The coffee was good. It was a luxury. The Vasaanens had few luxuries. Not that they couldn't afford them but after spending all the formative years being frugal it was a little uncomfortable being anything else. Franz had once remarked that he felt guilty when they had things like coffee; as though he were doing something not quite nice nor honest.

Tonight he drank his coffee without conscious effort. Its tonic-effect was lacking. After a while Marta suggested bed and he agreed. They lay awake in the hushed darkness, he with his canker, she conscious of his weight at her side, of his breathing, of the little moan that escaped him even after sleep came. She cried silently on her side of the bed.

Wooden houses made little rustling noises with each change of temperature. The wood which expanded in warm daytime, contracted in the chill of night. Sometimes one of the little winds in off the Joki's estuary, not too distant, brushed heavy fingers over rooftops and people lying awake listened.

For Helene the night was endless. She slept early then awakened with the chill coming through her screenless window. The house was 'working' as the older people said; it was making those little living sounds. She lay abed feeling a little sick, feeling she'd done a frightful thing to her parents. But that night below town she'd forgot her parents completely. Had forgot everything in fact except her love.

Now she'd had a month to reflect and all the things she hadn't been the least aware of then, came up to face her now. They kept coming; first the sickness, then the gloom as realization dawned, then the panic, then the resolve, the wilfulness, the insistence that what she'd done might not be condoned by others but that in her own eyes it was too beautiful to be ugly or mean. Finally, the conviction that her child would be hers no matter what sacrifices she'd have to make to make this be so.

Then, the most demoralizing of all, the looks of her parents when they knew. That was what haunted her now, with the little cold breeze coming through her upstairs window.

Guilt rode her spirit hard. It did not ameliorate her personal feelings but it crushed her with its accusations and its pitiless recollections of how her mother had first acted and now, tonight, her father.

He'd seemed almost to fall apart. As though the shame were unbearable, yes, but more than that, as though she had betrayed him — the last person on earth he'd ever expected to do that to him.

She clenched both fists and tried to hold back the flooding tears but they came anyway. She turned into her pillow, buried her face and let go. Spasms shook her making the bed groan and squeak.

She loved her parents, had always loved them. Even when it had annoyed her over the years to hear them use the term *'German!'* as she knew their parents had used the term Russian, she still loved them even for their unreasoning illogic; she understood what was behind their implacable loathing. She'd heard from Eric Vendson, from old Einer when he'd been alive, from many of the older people why that hatred was so deep and abiding. She also knew something that if her parents understood it they never indicated this was so: every generation has its haunting memory of spoilers, of reavers. For her parents it was Germans.

But to her a German was a person; a nation, a place, in one exquisite moment it had been a

42

beautiful man with bright blue eyes and perfect features, with broad shoulders and suntanned arms and legs. The only thing that had seemed foreign had been communication. She knew no German, he knew so very little Finnish that they'd spoken in English, in which both were fluent. Otherwise, Hans Einhorst was a man to her, one to whom she'd given all her love and from whom she'd accepted all his love in return.

She had always known he would go away so that hadn't bowed her with grief, but she also knew something — she hadn't told her parents — he'd said he would return as soon as he could decently get clear of the tour.

Only now she hoped he wouldn't for two reasons. One; because of what her parents might do. Two; she didn't want him to know of this — other thing. She had no wish to see him look stricken and conscience-ridden, nor have him feel obligated.

What she had shared with him was sweeter than life, more wonderful than dreaming, more tender than music. It would become sordid the minute he became practical and honourable. She didn't want it damaged by anything like that.

When the tears stopped finally, shortly before dawn but with a paleness off across the black tree-tops presaging the new day, she arose, washed her hot face, then stood by the window and said a little prayer for all of them. After that she crawled back into bed and slept like the dead.

Her mother climbing the stairs awakened her, finally, and she got up just as the little rap came upon the door. She felt rested but drained dry. 'Right away,' she called quietly through the door. 'I'll be down right away, Mother.'

CHAPTER FIVE

A Raid!

'It was like something I once read in a book about the old-time Danes,' said Jannes Wilko, the farmer who had been robbed and nearly killed, and whose freehold was a big clearing east of the village. 'It was so quietly done I had no idea until someone made a noise and I raised up in bed — and there he was, big and shaggy, standing right beside me with a pistol pointed into my face.

'I hadn't heard a thing, I swear to you, until that moment, and by then it was almost over. I was rigid in among the blankets. You realize how it is — a man first opens his eyes, they don't focus right away. The shape was there, the head and shoulders, the arms and leg, the gun, but it was so dark in the room.'

Eric growled from the wall-bench of Franz's store. 'What did he say, Jannes?'

'Something. I didn't understand it. But I understood the pistol. I lay back feeling as though I couldn't catch my breath.'

'A German,' opined Trygve Vesainen. 'They've never come this close to Joki before though. Jannes; how many were there?'

'When they came inside, the one in the bedroom made us get up. My wife almost fainted with fright. They ordered her to feed them. At

45

that time I counted them. In my kitchen stood seven of them. There were others outside because I heard them moving around and sometimes saying something.'

'Saying what?' Eric wanted to know.

Jannes was a burly, barrel-chested grizzled, grey man with wrinkles round his eyes emanating in all directions. 'I told you,' he said. 'I didn't understand them.'

'Was it Swedish?'

'No of course not or I'd have understood some of it.'

'Russian, Jannes?'

'Well; my wife says some of the talk was in Russian, she should know having come across to us after the war. But some of them spoke in . . . I'm not certain of this . . . German.'

Gunnar Mainpaa let all his breath out, turned and gazed at Franz Vasaanen with whom he'd gone down to Raanujarvï ten days before. Franz looked pale everywhere but around the eyes; up there he looked darkly shadowed and slack. Franz was listening to each word Jannes Wilko related with an odd expression of grim conviction and bleak triumph.

Gunnar said, 'Franz . . . ?'

Vasaanen nodded. 'This time I think we should go after them.' He said that very quietly but with a coldness none of the others missed. 'Keep going after them until it is finished once and for all. Hunt them down. Eh, Eric?'

Vendson nodded without taking his eyes off

46

Jannes. Gunnar made a wry little face as he studied Franz. Always before Franz had thundered and denounced, usually the army or the government; he'd never been so quietly fierce as he was this time. Never before had he come right out and advocated what he now had proposed, stripping the village of its able-bodied men and making a real war against the Germans. It troubled Gunnar. He didn't like the idea of anyone making a personal vendetta out of this. In the end he said, 'The authorities down at Raanujarvï must be notified.'

Eric lifted pale, expressionless eyes. 'What for?' he wanted to know. '*This* time I say we do it all ourselves.'

Gunnar repudiated that with mild anger. 'You know very well there are laws which must be obeyed, Eric.'

The big Swede snorted and sat up straighter on his chair. 'Those laws help *them*, not us. Franz Vasaanen is right. We go after them and keep going. We put an end to these people as we should have done five years ago.'

Trygve murmured agreement. So did all the others excepting Jannes and he hadn't got over his fright yet. He said, 'They were going to shoot us. While they ate our food at the kitchen table they said they probably should shoot us.'

Gunnar said, 'I thought you had trouble understanding them.'

Jannes' eyes got perfectly round. 'You could understand that much, Gunnar, when they'd look at us and hold their guns, chewing like cattle with death all over their faces.'

'You also said they didn't allow you to use a light.'

Jannes began to frown a little, annoyed by what certainly seemed to him as though his veracity were under attack.

'There was a moon last night, Gunnar. There was enough light through the windows.'

Mainpaa then said, 'You'll come down to Raanujarvï with me, Jannes, and see if you can identify any of them for the police.'

Eric stood up. 'Talk,' he growled. 'That's always been the trouble. I've told you before — I can trace those men. I've done it time and time again. But alone I had to come back. This time we'll go in numbers, and we'll corner them. I know that forest.'

Gunnar sat gazing at the big Swede. Eric was a man it was difficult to feel comfortable with unless one talked of things which interested only Vendson. He was indifferent to the life of Joki. He cared little for the stores, the farms, the fishing, the logging, even the social affairs; he thought of hunting, it was true, which they all enjoyed more or less, but hunting with Eric Vendson was like setting forth to purposefully kill only for that purpose. It was grim and exhausting and had no sense of accomplishment at day's end. Franz himself had once said that, but in Gunnar's view, Franz was different now too. It was puzzling; it was almost bewildering. He said nothing until they were all outdoors again away from Franz and Helene, who'd been at her desk listening. Then Gunnar said to Jannes Wilko, 'I don't like it. Everyone seems to have changed. To have been changing for a long while now. It gives me an uneasy feeling.'

Jannes neither knew nor especially cared what Gunnar meant. He simply said, 'Why were you trying to discredit me in there, Gunnar? I can show you my wife — she's still shaking. I left her with Marta Vasaanen. I can show you our kitchen, and also I can show you their bootprints in the soft earth. Not to mention the place from which they took my guns and ammunition and even the little money we had saved.'

Gunnar let Jannes get it all said, then laid a hand upon the burly farmer's arm, lowered his voice a little until it sounded melancholy, and explained as best he could that while he of course believed the Wilkos had been robbed the night before, he wasn't so sure it was the Germans. 'Look at it this way, Jannes; for twenty years they've been out there. They've been hungry before. But never have they bothered a village.'

'Well who was it then; there is nothing on the wireless about Finland being invaded. Anyway, they weren't soldiers.'

Gunnar looked doleful. 'All right. It was the Germans. But I don't like what's happening here now; everyone listening to old Eric. We could have a lot of us killed, Jannes. Those men are woodsmen; after all these years they've got to be. What are we?'

'Finns,' muttered the burly farmer, braver now in hot sunlight. 'With Eric leading we'll get them. It's about time too. And I agree with Eric; what have the police or the army ever done except shrug us off? Well then . . .'

'Come,' said Gunnar with resignation. 'We'll borrow Trygve's car.'

When the store was finally empty Franz kept leaning on his counter looking out the door where a golden span of summer sunlight lay in the roadway-dust. Helene waited for him to turn, to speak. He didn't do it. She said, 'Isn't it better to leave this to the police, father?'

His shoulders bunched a little but he didn't turn right away. Still gazing ahead he answered quietly, dully, 'It's been left to the police before, Helene. I agree with Eric. This is enough. Everyone knows they are in the forest. The army has known for years. So have the police. No one does anything.'

'But you've said yourself —'

He turned to face her and the words drifted off into heavy silence. He looked straight at her with an odd light in his eyes. He wouldn't have heard what she'd said even if she'd completed saying it. She went back to work on the books.

Eric came by shortly before closing time to drop his head low like a conspirator and say something in a low growl to Franz. Helene's father nodded and went to the ammunition closet, counted out seven cartons and handed them over. No money exchanged hands. Helene waited until Eric had departed under his burden then said, 'How do I enter that transaction since no bill will come across my desk for it?'

Franz pursed his lips, glanced at his watch and said serenely, 'It is ten minutes until closing time. Let's just lock up and go home.' He made no allusion to the ammunition at all and Helene, who knew her father, did not mention it again.

Marta had supper ready as always. It was a dull, crushing meal even though Marta struggled to make it otherwise. Later, when Franz took his hat and left the house, Marta turned an anxious face to her daughter.

'They're going after the men in the forest,' Helene explained. 'Eric will lead them. Father gave him seven cartons of ammunition this afternoon. Mother; they shouldn't go — not the men as old as father.'

Marta nodded. She'd heard the entire episode of the Wilko raid from Jannes's wife herself, and on top of her other worries this one now lay pre-eminent since she realized her own husband was implicated.

'Helene; when you are my age and your husband does something young men might do — say nothing.'

'Even if he gets himself killed, Mother?'

Marta thought she knew the answer, for although she'd never lost a husband she knew how a man's mind would work on that question. 'I suppose even then,' she said, and arose to clear away the dishes. From the kitchen doorway she suddenly turned and said. 'Heaven prevent it,' and then moved out of sight.

Franz did not return home until very late and in his absence Trygve Vesainen came by looking for him. Helene said dryly, 'Try Eric Vendson's house.' Still later, when he still hadn't returned, Gunnar came round looking stooped and weary. He also wished to see Franz. Helene gave him the same suggestion, then leaned upon the door-jamb and gazed at the man she'd known since babyhood. 'Uncle; did you see the police down in Raanujarvï?'

'Yes. They will send up a patrol to investigate.' Gunnar pulled a face. 'If half the village were murdered they would send two patrols. But I went to the army.'

'They will come?'

'In a sense, Helene; they will send wireless messages to an outpost on the other side of the forest to move in with force and perhaps catch the Germans between our force and theirs.'

'Our force,' murmured Helene. 'Uncle; my father nor you nor most of the others can go three hundred miles through the forest with little to eat and perhaps no rest — and perhaps get yourselves ambushed by those renegades.'

Gunnar didn't argue the point. He simply said what was obvious. 'Eric will lead them and they will go, Helene. No one could stop them now. I've thought for a long time the killing of young

Gust Eisen might make them do this. When it didn't I was gratified. But now they will go. And I realize what you say is true enough — but if you told your father that he would say you were mistaken; that he did it once before and he can do it again.'

'Can't you stop them, Uncle?'

'Helene; I can't stop them. I'm going with them.' Gunnar made a tired little grin. 'I'm older than most of them so perhaps when my legs fail I won't have so far to walk back. But they are right in a little way; this whole thing has dragged on long enough. If the army moves in from the far side of the forest this may be the best chance we'll ever have to put an end to it. Well; when your father returns tell him I'll be ready in the morning to accompany them. Good night.'

She watched his shambling walk and wanted to cry out that he was mad to even think of going with the others, but from behind her Marta, who'd heard it all, said, 'Remember what I told you?'

Helene remembered. She closed the door, went back to her chair and sat down. All of a sudden her own problem seemed less towering, less overpowering. She gazed at her mother, who might lose her man. Marta was at the knitting again, something she never did during the summers, only during the winters. Helene watched her mother's face and tried to guess what was going on behind the lowered, narrowed eyes. She failed.

CHAPTER SIX

Return Of The German

The most unsettling event of all occurred the very next morning when Marta and Helene were up early preparing breakfast while Franz, who'd already left the house to make last-minute preparations before they'd arisen, was gone.

The mother of the dead Eisen boy came across to say her husband was going and wring her hands about that. But at least he had a personal vendetta which the women, although disapproving, could readily understand.

They gave her black coffee, did as much reassuring as they could and sent her back home. Otherwise there was nothing they could do.

Franz returned with the sun. In cool morning he did, in fact, look younger and step lighter. He had a Luger pistol belted round his middle beneath the jacket and was wearing sturdy boots. While he wolfed down food and Helene made up a pack for him of additional provender, Marta asked when he might return. He didn't know; perhaps it wouldn't take very long. He thought that if the soldiers moved quickly in from the lower end of the forest, and if the brigands didn't know they were coming, it just might work out very well.

Helene was practical. 'They'll know,' she said.

'It's foolish to think men who've been in the forest for so many years won't know how to take every precaution.'

Franz's answer was short and full of grim conviction. 'Eric also knows the forest.'

Helene finished the packet and took it to her father with a solemn expression. She stooped and kissed his cheek without saying anything. He looked up, watched her turn away.

Marta fussed a little. 'Well; surely you men will have Trygve's car take the loads, won't you? What's the point in burdening yourselves with heavy packs?' Marta was thinking of their aged legs and physically soft bodies.

Franz finished eating, arose and looked at his wife. Marta was a hard-worker. For a woman she was very rational. Of course having come to maturity in grim times she'd become almost man-like in many ways. But she was a good mother, an excellent cook, a real comfort. He took her hand and walked her out to the doorway with him.

'I may not get the right German,' he confided, 'but I'll get *a* German.'

Marta was resigned but also exasperated. She understood why he was doing this; she also thought it was very foolish. Not going after the brigands who'd raided the Wilko's place, nor even wanting blood for the brigandage, but for him in particular and other older men to make the effort. There were enough younger men in the village. But she acted according to her private knowledge of her man and nodded dumbly at him. She would not argue, she would simply send him on his way with her best wishes and silent prayers.

When they parted Franz took up his pack, the rifle he'd discreetly left beside the door outside, and walked down towards the centre of the village where other men were milling, talking, smoking, making last-minute inventories of their burdens amid a silent, still group of village onlookers, mostly women and young children.

There were about forty of them. Some were young and strong. It was about equally divided between youth and age, this expedition. There would be perhaps twice as many men who would not be going off, generally older and wiser, or handicapped some way so that they couldn't go.

Eric was there, big and erect and muscular, looking and acting much younger than he must be and wearing a light knitted hat of very dark blue — the kind of headgear called by American sailors a 'watch cap' and in fact he'd got it from an American sailor.

They had good guns, for although private ownership of weapons was viewed askance by officialdom, being villagers on the outskirts of a big forest, no real issue had ever actually been made of this matter. Marta wished now the issue had been made, but wishing never accomplished very much.

The men had two automobiles; these left first by the westerly road. Eric took the armed party along in their wake and within a very short time they all faded out in the trees. Marta stood watching as long as any were in sight, then, when Helene joined her outside, they watched the villagers down there acting like leaderless sheep. Helene said she had to go open the store. Marta was bleak about that.

'There'll be no customers today. Look at them; whimpering children and weeping women. I have a very bad feeling about this.'

Helene patted her mother and left, walking down towards the village's small, compact business section. Marta watched that departure too, and was grim about the proud way her daughter strode along — her *pregnant* daughter — as though she didn't know the meaning of the word Shame.

Fortunately, there was much work to be done round the house for otherwise Marta might have given way to the tears which were beginning to mist her vision as she turned heavily to go indoors.

It was a beautiful day. Not too warm for a change, but not cold either. Occasionally such a day came, along towards the end of summer or before, to remind people that winter would return.

Ordinarily such a day was welcomed. It showed by osmosis that people were attuned to the changes, the equinoxes; that civilization, only three or four thousand years old, hadn't taken the place of natural things to which people responded without always realizing they were doing so. But not today although people did seem to move about more, but as Helene observed from the store, it was a restless, fuddled, directionless kind of movement.

There was little enough trade, as her mother had predicted and women shoppers had something to say about the men going off. They also had bitter comments to make about a government which sat hundreds of miles southward busy with the ramifications of internationalism while the people with whom they *should* be concerned were fighting a silent war no one as far off as Helsinki seemed to know about, or care about.

Kasimir Mainpaa, Gunnar's nephew with the curved spine and bitter eyes that tried to smile and never actually succeeded, lingered at the empty counter to accuse the army of caring very little about the northern countryside and preferring to drink and roister in the towns. Kasimir was a student; not in the sense that others were students. He was thirty years of age which was past the time for going to school, but since his deformity made it difficult for him to do anything physical, he read books. History and geography mainly, but any kind of book he got his hands on. He was versed in all the things most country people knew little or nothing about, unless of course personal destiny had thrust events upon them. It was Kasimir who'd stung the people to anger several years earlier when they'd lost that alien schoolmaster by saying that whether his ideas were valid or not, at least his progressive attitude was refreshing. Kasimir's uncle had been so resentful he'd scarcely spoken to his nephew for a year afterwards.

But Kasimir's mind was sharp and penetrating, as now when he told Helene what the men had done was absolutely idiotic, for although the government and the army would do nothing, it still wasn't the responsibility of a bunch of old men to hasten forth to fight experienced woodsmen.

For the sake of argument and to break the monotony of an empty store, she'd said that, right or wrong, at least the men had finally taken the initiative instead of leaving it always with the Germans.

That had stung Kasimir. 'Germans? Helene, you're talking like *them*, like the older people. Germans! The enemy of Finland has always been Russia, not Germany. How many times have the Russians over-run us; how many cities and ports have they taken from us; how many thousands of our people have they stolen and used for slaves, or killed, or plundered?'

Helene was a girl; she remembered only vague bits of the history she'd learned in school. Besides, history had never interested her at all, so when Kasimir, failing to elicit a worthwhile answer, stalked out of the store she was glad for his departure and returned to the desk.

Fifteen minutes later she felt a presence although no one had entered the room or the little bell would have tinkled on the door. She looked up and her breath stopped.

He smiled from the doorway and said, 'I couldn't catch the others.' He stepped inside, his quiet eyes and sensitive lips smiling. 'I didn't really try very hard anyway.'

She started breathing again but with a queer feeling in her breast. He *was* beautiful. Handsome didn't describe him at all. The fair, curly hair, the perfect, flawless features, the wide shoulders, slim hips, bronzed arms and legs, the light step and easy assurance.

'Hans,' she whispered it.

He leaned across the counter. 'You act as though you didn't think I'd return, Helene. I told you I would as soon as I could get away from the tour.'

Her legs were too weak to support her so she continued to sit behind the desk. The queerness spread all through her. She was light-headed. She wanted him terribly and yet she also didn't want him. It was confusing and vexatious to feel that way because ordinarily she knew her mind very well.

He kept watching her, his smile thinning down. 'You don't want me here, Helene; you thought I wouldn't come back, that I didn't mean the things I said?'

She shook her head. 'I believed you, Hans.'

'Then why do you look that way?'

She unconsciously raised a hand to her face. It

was cold. She stammered something and forced herself to arise, to cross to him at the counter. The moment he reached and touched her the warmth flooded back through her. She *did* want him. No matter about her secret now, she wanted him more than life itself.

She began speaking, not calmly at all but pushing words out, telling him of the departure of the men after those brigands in the forest everyone said were Germans. It had nothing to do with what lay between them, personally, but she spoke compulsively, almost defensively, while her mind went its private way: if he stayed in Joki of course he was going to find out her secret, but if she sent him away, she would certainly die of the loss.

He let her talk for a long while, then lay a strong hand upon her arm and shook his head at her. 'We heard there were brigands in this north country, but Helene, they don't have much to do with us, do they?'

'My father went with the others, Hans.'

'Oh.' He removed the hand and looked at the top of the counter. Eventually he said, 'Why do you call them Germans?'

She hadn't as a matter of fact used that designation but obviously since he'd heard of the brigands, he'd also heard them called that. She said, 'It's not entirely clear to me about that, except that the older people say Finland's most recent troubles were caused by the Germans. Hans; it's just a term they use.'

He nodded a trifle solemnly. 'Sometimes, since I've been on the tour, I've thought it would have been better to have been born two or three generations from now when the things that happened thirty years ago would have been replaced in people's minds by other, different things, which will happen in the years ahead.' He looked enquiringly at her. 'Do you follow me?'

She loved him. When he spoke or dropped his head or lifted his eyes or smiled or frowned or touched her or simply stood there listening, she could feel a kind of insular ecstasy that approximated the other ecstasy he brought to her. She nodded without knowing exactly what he'd said.

Jannes Wilko ambled in and stood irresolutely looking at them. Jannes hadn't gone with the others even though he'd seemed to want to. Now, as Helene moved along the counter he shuffled over, asked for tobacco, which she got for him, and he turned a little so that he could study Hans Einhorst, an obvious stranger. But he said nothing and after paying for his tobacco shuffled out again.

Helene's mind finally recovered, turned cool and rational as she went back where Hans waited. 'None of the others returned with you, Hans?'

'No. In fact I only found two of them — sore-legged stragglers. I told them I was coming back; asked them to tell the tour-leader I was leaving the group and would return home by myself.'

'Are you camped south of the village?'

He nodded.

'Then wait for me tonight.'

He nodded again, searching her face, but when he might have spoken she reached with a cool hand and touched his cheek. He then braced far over the counter and met her lips coming inward. She pulled back almost at once for fear someone might come into the store, her cheeks flaming red. She smiled.

'Go now, and I'll be down as soon as I can decently get there. And Hans . . .'

'Yes.'

'Do you really — still . . . ?'

'More than ever, Helene. So much more than ever it's all I can think about.'

He briskly walked out of the store leaving a silence behind so profound she was steeped in it.

CHAPTER SEVEN

Footsteps In The Night

Marta was fretful and garrulous when Helene arrived home that evening with the sun still high. 'Why didn't they send someone back to let us know where they are?' she mumbled as they worked side by side in the kitchen preparing a meal neither of them felt the least desire for. 'And suppose they find the Germans and provoke them into real anger against Joki? It's possible the Germans will then come back here because they'll know most of the worthwhile men are out in the forest.'

Helene had to force herself by a very real effort to hear her mother. She also had to concentrate on what her hands were doing. She wanted to cry out that Hans was back. Instead she simply said, 'We'll hear, Mother. And if they find those men I doubt if they'll try coming here. That wouldn't be very wise. Moreover, they have hundreds of miles of forest to hide in. I know that father and the others hid out there during the war but that was a long while ago and the brigands are fresher at that sort of thing. It wouldn't surprise me at all if father didn't see a single brigand.'

'I hope so,' breathed Marta, somewhat relieved by Helene's practical, calm words. 'I certainly hope all they get is sore feet and aching backs.'

They ate, both of them forcing the food down. The sun was stubborn about setting this night, or so it seemed to Helene who looked up now and then from the table until Marta asked if she'd heard something, and after that Helene just ate.

The excuse was a valid one and should have aroused no suspicion in any event because it was used frequently enough; Helene had some work to do at the store. She flinched as she said it because lying was difficult for her and under no stretch of the imagination could this be called anything but a lie. Marta accepted it and that hurt too. It wasn't a matter of deceiving her mother so much as it was a matter of being believed when she hadn't told the truth that troubled Helene. It's never hard to lie to someone who believes in a person.

The night was pleasant, not as warm as the nights had been but still quite benign. There was a small moon, thin and weak, but the brilliant stars made up for that. Also, as Helene walked down through the village, she glimpsed lighted windows, heard radios tuned up in the stillness, and saw several people also strolling the night whom she managed to avoid without trouble, at least she thought she'd avoided them, but then since she was walking southward and there was someone behind her, she had no idea at all she'd been observed. Even if she'd known, perhaps she'd have paid scant attention because Jannes Wilko was no one who fitted into her world in any event. Furthermore, when she left the village and walked in the direction of the hostel and camp-ground southward, Jannes turned in at the house of Trygve Vesainen, who was with the men in the forest, so he didn't actually see how far below town she went.

Hans was waiting beneath a huge old tree whose limbs had been cut away for a distance of perhaps twenty feet from the ground. He was dressed in light-coloured cotton trousers and a short-sleeved, open-collared shirt of the same shade which made his throat and face and strong arms look darker than ever. She said he looked like an Italian or perhaps a Spaniard, although she'd only seen a few of the former and none of the latter. He flashed her a smile and said, 'I thought you might say I looked older; I've been waiting all day.'

He took her hand and led her away from the dark little log hostel, built by the community to accommodate touring students, down along a well-trod path towards a rill of water that came down-country and inland from the river, to a glade she vividly remembered. He would have stopped there but she didn't want to. It seemed wrong to be there now. She tugged at him going farther along until the ground turned marshy, like a muskeg swamp, and there, where their path branched off she led him northward as though she were familiar with all this, which she was; which in fact was where she'd often played as a child because the pathway terminated where a number of fishing boats had been hauled up and over-turned along the shore, looking very much like hump-backed slumbering whales in the starlight.

Here, the river touched land, and trees stood back a respectful distance leaving a strip of wiry grass and round-leaved, ground-hugging plants similar to seagrape.

The moon was above, the stars glowed, and a breath of steady coolness came inland from the river which was wide and sluggish at this point, with islets faintly discernible far out. She said, 'It floods every spring,' as though they'd come here just to consider this phenomenon. 'I've even heard people say that once in a while it comes right to the edge of the village although I've never seen that. But when it freezes you can skate for miles. . . .' She turned. He was standing there gazing quietly at her profile, which was sturdy and good in the tinny light.

She felt for his hand. It was warm. She turned to gaze upwards. He seemed very solemn so she smiled a little with her lips and squeezed his fingers. He squeezed back.

'Well . . .' he murmured, and stopped, took down a breath and started again. 'Well; I don't know how to say the things I've been thinking lately but I'll try. I can't get you out of my mind, Helene.'

Her smile died. 'Did you try?'

He released her hand, looked at the water, looked back again. 'No. Not really. But — it's like everything before just ended. Just stopped being — stopped existing. I came on this tour to see Scandinavia. That's all. I had no idea at all anything else would happen. Then it happened — and everything that went before just suddenly ended. Last week a college boy — this week a man in every way that counts.' He made a futile small gesture with his hands. 'I can't explain it, even. I'm not saying how I feel or what I know.'

'Hans; what do you know?'

'I'm in love, Helene. I know that. And that's something else; I've been in love before. Well; maybe not really, but it seemed like love until now — until last week and the week before and all the way back to that first time I was with you. It interferes with everything I do, Helene.'

'You don't want it to?'

He looked at her almost in exasperation. 'Stop trying to make me say I regret things.'

She searched roundabout for a tussock of salt-grass, found one and sat down upon it looking at the silvery run of water. He growled something under his breath and sank down beside her.

'Forgive me. I didn't mean to be short with you, Helene. But this isn't anything I can just sit and think through to a neat conclusion.'

He waited for her to speak, to turn her head, to move at all. She didn't do any of those things. A little tumbling breeze came to stir the curls of her hair, to riffle the hem of her skirt. Then it passed and she reminded him of a little bronze maiden he'd seen in Norway who sat on a boulder near the sea. Only the little bronze maiden had no clothes on and she was looking downward not outward. He reached. Her arm was cool velvet.

'In college I go out with girls. We laugh a lot and dance or sing.'

'And that's all, Hans?'

They were the first words she'd spoken in something like fifteen minutes so he was waiting for them. But even then he didn't answer her.

'But with you it was different right from the start. I didn't want to share you with anyone; I didn't want to sit and sing or jump up and dance. I just wanted to see you — touch you — be alone with you.'

She turned, her expression sober, her eyes, blue by daylight, nearly black now. 'Is that all?'

He didn't catch the implication but he said, 'No; but are we old enough — ready — for bigger things? I still have a year more of college. After that I'll have no job, or at the very best. only a minor position somewhere.' His eyes were pleading but she couldn't supply any of the answers because she didn't know them, wasn't even aware they existed, and didn't care whether they existed or not.

She kept gazing down at him.

He tried a smile that didn't quite come off. 'Marriage, Helene?'

'You aren't ready, Hans?'

'God yes I'm ready,' he blurted out.

She wilted a little where she sat, her dark eyes beginning to catch a glimpse of his torment. She almost soothed him by saying, 'We should wait,' then she thought of something else and didn't respond with any words at all.

He returned her steady look. 'Did it strike you like this, Helene?'

She nodded. It had struck her like this yes, only it had struck her so much harder that she'd done a terrible thing without even once considering the consequences.

'And tell me, Helene; what do you think?'

She couldn't say what she thought. She didn't want him to know what she knew or he'd be stunned and ashamed and under an immediate and irrefutable obligation. Or else he might run away and she didn't want to know that he'd do that either.

'Tell me,' he insisted.

She shook her head at him returning the initiative intact because she didn't want it. Whatever he said or did he must do by himself. She felt miserable, half wishing she hadn't come down to see him because even if he said the right things now, and she told him the secret it would still hit him like a great blow. She felt almost a sudden, hot loathing for her body.

He tried a lighter mood. 'Love does odd things to a man; one minute he wants to spring up and shout to the world, the next minute he wants to sit under a tree and brood.' He smiled upwards. 'I suppose it's different with a girl but it can't be very different. We're not all that different. Anyway, you're just enough different. You're soft and strong and beautiful . . .' he ended a little breathlessly. 'I hate poetry. Always have, probably because in school we had to study it. But at least now I can see how men have written the stuff.'

She felt tears coming and sprang off the grass facing the river. With all the things he said which touched her, he still hadn't said the right thing. 'We'd better go back,' she murmured, turning away without facing him.

He arose, dusted himself and took two big steps to catch her. 'Wait. We haven't decided anything, Helene.'

'What is there to decide, Hans? You have to finish your schooling don't you?'

'I suppose so. At least if I stopped attending now my parents would —'

'Then what is there to discuss?'

'This,' he growled, and swung her to him, caught her close and kissed her with a hurting insistence. She fought free, pale and trembling.

'No,' she said flatly. 'No.'

His arms dropped, his brow knit, his eyes began to discern something he hadn't seen before. He eventually said, 'You are ashamed, Helene.'

She didn't reply for a moment but eventually she did. 'No, Hans. I'm not ashamed. I loved you and you loved me.'

'Past tense?' he asked a trifle sharply.

'Not past tense. I still love you. I probably always shall. But what good can come of any of it? You have to return to Essen and to school.'

'But I'll come back next summer.'

She bit her lip, waited a moment then, forcing her voice to be calm, said, 'No; next summer will be too . . . well . . . next summer is a long way off and maybe we'll both be changed by then.'

He started to protest, to reach again, but she was swift in avoiding both his touch and words. She fled back along the pathway.

She got all the way back to the little log hostel without hearing him pursuing her, but she was out of breath when she reached it so had to pause a moment in the gloomy shadows of that de-limbed big old tree for a moment, until she heard his angry steps, then she ran on again, this time heading blindly back up towards the village, sobs tearing at her throat, scalding tears obscuring her vision so badly that she didn't see Jannes Wilko stop up in front of Trygve Vesainen's place, and look after her in frank astonishment until she was gone, then Jannes turned and slowly looked southward where a tall, broad-shouldered man, very easily seen because of his white attire, stood halfway up towards the village, hands on hips, head thrown back, listening to the diminishing footfalls far ahead.

Jannes watched the tall youth for a long while, until Hans turned and went loosely shuffling back down towards the log hostel, then Jannes leaned upon Trygve's wooden fence beside the roadway and raised a thick hand to perplexedly scratch his head. In the end, he turned and headed for the house of curved-back Kasimir Mainpaa. It was still early in the night. There was a light from Kasimir's parlour.

CHAPTER EIGHT

By Stealth In The Night

Kasimir listened in genuine surprise then he said, leaning upon the table with the big book spread open beneath his elbows, 'But if you saw her walk down there earlier, then possibly she was meeting this man. You also said he looked like the same person you saw earlier in the store, Jannes.'

Jannes had no answers to refute Kasimir's imputations with so all he said was, 'Why was she running so hard to get away from him, then, and why was she crying? No; he waylaid her as I said — she went for a walk and this man waylaid her. He didn't try going up through the village after her, Kasimir. He was fearful of doing that for otherwise she might have screamed for help.'

Kasimir slowly leaned back off the table, his crooked back blending perfectly with the specially constructed chair. He stared at Jannes. 'We can't just walk up and knock on Vasaanen's door and ask if this stranger molested her, Jannes.'

'No,' agreed the farmer with a wolfish grin. 'But we *can* get one or two others and sneak down there at the hostel and ask *him*, Kasimir.'

For a man who was neither physically endowed nor supposedly intellectually inclined towards violence Kasimir Mainpaa agreed with

74

alacrity. 'I'll get Alexis Kanth and Eino Kurikka. You go down and spy. Make certain this man is still down there.'

They parted out front of Kasimir's house, Jannes heading southward after a final whispered consultation out of which came the agreement that Jannes was to do nothing except locate the stranger, then meet Kasimir, Eino and Alexis up the roadway.

For Jannes the route was easy, the undertaking simple. Hans Einhorst was not hiding from anyone. In fact when Jannes first spotted him he was standing near a bicycle tying a bundle behind the seat. Jannes interpreted this to mean the stranger was about to climb astride and ride away. With his heart in his mouth and dozens of shallow but heroic ideas flashing through his mind, he cursed Kasimir's slowness. He didn't particularly choose to jump the tall, broad-shouldered stranger by himself although if need be he would do so.

But Hans resolved things by turning after a bit and going over beside the log hostel where a sleeping bag had been unfurled. Jannes had been so busy watching the bicycle he'd neglected to see the sleeping bag. Now he loosened all over and sighed in silence.

Hans sat on the bag. He was wearing low cloth shoes with white laces which he started to remove. Jannes smiled to himself, turned and started silently away. He met Kasimir and the other two a hundred rods away looking anxious and furtive. He informed them the stranger was readying for bed; that if they split up, two approaching from around the far side of the log structure, two from the near side, they'd have him before he could jump up and run.

Kasimir and Eino went off to the right, Jannes and Alexis went stealthily down towards the left side, or front, of the hostel-building. The moon fell behind some high clouds but before long it slid back out again. Not that they needed its light, they knew every inch of the way and every yard of the surrounding countryside as well.

Eino Kurikka was a flat-faced, slant-eyed, stocky, grinning man with bad teeth and eyes that were a very unique shade of blue-black. He wasn't thought — or at least *said* — to be a Laplander, but he certainly looked like one.

Alexis Kanth drank and did very little work although professing to be a boat-builder, which Trygve Vesainen also was, except that Trygve actually built boats while Alexis talked about building boats. He was part Russian; his father by his own boasts, had been a Russian soldier who'd fought his way into Finland during the Russian-Finnish War back before the Second World War. Alexis was not a popular man in Joki and it didn't altogether have to do with his drinking; he was also a whiner. When the winters were severe he rarely had enough wood put by. When the boats were out, he always had a leaky craft, or his nets were torn. None of it was ever his fault.

He was a brutish man with a coarse, round face, thick neck, and had the strength of a bull despite the fact that he hadn't been a young man for many years.

When he came round the hostel with Jannes, who was also physically compact and powerful, to face Hans Einhorst, Alexis grinned broadly at the startled expression of the sitting youth.

Kasimir and Eino stepped up too, thus cutting off flight for Hans, who, shoeless, slowly got up to his feet looking at the weird assortment of cripples and brutes surrounding him in the cooling night.

Kasimir hitched up closest and peered. 'Who are you?' he asked in Finnish, and at the blank look, he tried again in Swedish, then in such terrible Russian that Alexis snorted and put the question more properly in Russian. Hans looked blank. Eino, studying the tall youth intently, suddenly growled out the question in guttural German and at once Hans answered, looking at Eino only.

'My name is Hans Einhorst. I am from Essen in Germany.'

The men who didn't understand the words nevertheless understood what language was being spoken. They stood like stone images regarding the tall youth. Jannes said, 'A German. By God he is a German!'

No one answered that statement. No one asked Hans another question for a long while, then Kasimir, nominal leader although Jannes had made the discovery, said, 'Why did you molest that girl; do you Germans still think you are a master race?'

Hans shrugged. He didn't understand enough Finnish to make sense of any of that. He said, switching to English which he knew was widely spoken in the North, 'I was with a student group touring the country.'

Even Alexis understood English although he had great difficulty speaking it. Not so Kasimir, the scholar, who'd had many a weary winter to perfect his use of the language. 'Where are the other students, then?' he asked.

Hans studied the hunchback a moment before replying. Kasimir seemed the most grotesque in the starlight, but he also seemed the most intelligent. 'They went on. I started to catch them — then came back.'

'Ahhh?' said Alexis, leering. 'Why did you come back?'

Hans switched his attention. It took no great experience to see the antagonism in this man. 'It's my private affair,' he told Kanth. The round-faced man curled both hands into fists and glared, but he said no more.

Kasimir did, though. 'You molested a girl. You were seen at it. Do you know what can happen to you for such an act?'

Hans, comprehension coming suddenly, let his jaw sag. He stared at all four of them. 'I didn't molest anyone.'

Jannes leaned slightly from the hips. This was

his charge; he did not mean for this German to wiggle out of it. 'I saw you. I saw her running and crying to escape from you.'

Hans's face twisted into an angry expression. 'You are a liar,' he said slowly, in English.

Jannes, still rocking forward, dropped his arms straight down. His narrowed eyes seemed to turn milky. He was prepared for quick violence but Kasimir intervened by saying, 'Einhorst; are you telling us you didn't touch this girl; are you saying she wasn't running from you, but from someone else?'

'I'm not saying anything,' Hans grated, still warily eyeing Jannes Wilko. 'If you think I molested her why don't you go and make certain I did such a thing before coming down here like this?'

'Well,' explained Kasimir, 'we can't just go up and ask a woman a thing like that, so we've come to hear your side of it.'

'And if I don't tell you my side of it?'

Alexis raised a meaty fist. 'You will tell us,' he promised.

Jannes, still poised, nodded agreement. 'Tell us now that you saw no girl; that there wasn't one down here. Tell these men that when I saw her running and crying I saw a ghost. Go on — they are waiting — tell them!'

Hans stood as tall as Alexis, who was the tallest of the Finns. He seemed to have completely overcome his earlier shock now. 'There was a girl,' he admitted, willing at last to speak

79

candidly. 'But I didn't molest her. In fact, we met down here. We met before, when I was visiting Joki before. If she was crying I didn't know it. We talked a little and walked back through the trees to where some little boats are beached. Then she had to leave. That's all. Go and ask her, she'll tell you. We have nothing to hide.'

Kasimir settled back a little as he studied the German youth's face. Jannes and Alexis were still belligerent but slightly less so. Eino put a cigarette in his mouth and lit it behind cupped hands. He was the only one there who smoked.

Kasimir made his decision. 'Those things tied on the bicycle — you were preparing to leave Joki?'

'In the morning,' said Hans, then, anticipating the next question, he said, 'If you wish I'll go with one of you to her house and you can ask if I bothered her in any way.'

Kasimir looked at Eino who blew fragrant smoke and said, 'Well; Jannes thought he saw something. It is understandable. But I'm not going to the house with the boy.'

Alexis looked uncertain now too; there was no denying Einhorst's sincerity. But Jannes, who would come out of this looking least heroic, said, 'I'll go. I still say she was running away from him and she was crying.'

Kasimir made the final decision. 'You will all stay here and watch his bicycle. I'll go with him. Then I'll bring him back.'

Hans stooped to pull on his cloth shoes. When

he straightened up he looked squarely at Jannes Wilko. 'You made a mistake, that's all. Maybe you were justified, seeing no more than you saw, but another man would have come alone instead of trying to make something criminal out of it.'

He then turned and strode off with crooked-back Kasimir Mainpaa leaving Jannes looking after him feeling very uncomfortable; in spite of himself he now was fairly confident he *had* made a mistake and it made him blush furiously as he turned to Eino and Alexis. 'She *was* crying and running away from him. I don't care what anyone says. I know what I saw.'

Kasimir too began to feel uneasy as they approached the darkened Vasaanen house. When they were directly out front his misgivings became acute. For one thing the German knew exactly which house it was. For another he'd strode along with full confidence. Finally, it began to bother Kasimir that if Helene knew this handsome youth, had voluntarily gone out to meet him at night and now Kasimir came up with some kind of very embarrassing question, Helene was going to be furious with him. Not only that, but her parents would be very angry too — and of course that would mean his own uncle would be furious as well.

He stopped Hans with a word, looked round at all the darkened houses, fidgeted, then said, 'Can you tell me anything to convince me Helene Vasaanen met you voluntarily?'

Hans thought a moment then said, 'That

short, weathered man down there — he saw us together in the store today. We were talking together when he came in for tobacco.'

'Eino?'

'No. The one called Jannes.'

Kasimir thought. 'For tobacco? Jannes doesn't smoke.'

'I can't say anything about that; today he bought tobacco at the store while Helene and I were talking. In fact that's when she agreed to meet me down by the hostel tonight.'

Kasimir, confronted with the ringing sincerity of the German, was face to face with another dilemma: why would Jannes Wilko buy tobacco if he didn't use it? Finally, wishing only to extricate himself from something that was becoming more intolerable with each passing moment, Kasimir said, 'Einhorst; I want your word you will meet me at Vasaanen's store in the morning so that I can see Helene when she sees you.'

Hans didn't hesitate. 'At nine o'clock on the hour,' he said, then, sensing the hunchback's dilemma, he looked up at the house and said, 'Molest her? Never in this life would I molest her.'

Kasimir, extricated but still feeling very uncomfortable, turned back. 'Stay up here,' he said. 'Or better yet, go round through the back of the village and down to your camp. That will give me time to disperse the others. If you see them you needn't say anything about your promise to meet me. I'll tell a different story to get rid of them.'

Hans watched the cripple scuttle back down the way he'd come, through the first real chill of night. It was by this time getting very close to midnight when the chill always came. He moved off, finally, following Kasimir Mainpaa's advice, but without looking the least bit pleased about what amounted to a deliverance.

CHAPTER NINE

Return Of Mainpaa And Vasaanen

Kasimir Mainpaa was correct. When Hans related what had occurred the night before, Helene was furious. But Hans was at the store a half hour early, therefore, when Kasimir walked in promptly at nine o'clock the roof nearly fell on him.

Helene didn't even give him an opportunity to explain. She said, 'Kasimir, I'm going to see that your uncle hears how you sneak about spying on people in the night. And my father as well. I'm going to tell everyone what an underhanded person you've become, probably peeking into windows at night too. Otherwise why were you and Jannes skulking about watching people last night?'

Kasimir looked at Hans, his expression twisted with chagrin. Hans offered him no help whatsoever. In fact, he appeared to enjoy the spectacle of Helene going after Kasimir. As soon as he decently could the cripple escaped. Helene, red and upset, went back behind the counter of the store, leaned there without looking at Hans and seemed again on the verge of tears. Hans told her it was really nothing; since the four men had done nothing physical, and since she'd just belaboured the cripple until he fled, the episode might be considered ended. For some reason he didn't fathom, and which increased his sensation of discomfort, Helene was not in the least placated. She went to her desk, kept her back to him and said, 'I never thought of that. Suppose this wasn't the first time — they spied?'

Hans understood finally, and was shocked. He looked at the doorway and beyond where morning light was strengthening, where a few people were abroad. Several sturdy children, half-grown and gabbling in their outlandish language, were hastening past. Two old men across the road were dolorously waggling their heads as they soberly conversed. Somewhere in the middle distance could be detected the sound of an automobile.

Helene, also picking up that sound, turned. The paleness of her face made the darkness of her shiny eyes more than ever noticeable. Hans watched as she began moving, slowly at first, then more swiftly, as she passed round the counter and headed for the doorway.

The automobile was dusty and lustreless as though it hadn't been travelling the throughways but had instead come a considerable distance over dirty roads. She recognized it about the same time a half dozen others also did. 'Trygve's car,' she said aloud, as Hans strolled over to stand there watching the auto approach. She ran outside. Hans remained where he was.

People appeared as though by magic, emptying from stores and houses to greet Trygve Vesainen when he halted his car, set the brake, opened the door and got out with a heaviness, a lethargy to his movements one ordinarily associated with much older men. In the rear seat were Gunnar Mainpaa, a filthy bandage about his head and left hand, Franz Vasaanen with a splinted leg, the spruce limbs of the splint extending below the booted foot so that Franz could navigate, and two more passengers, but they'd been folded over to fit inside the closed doors because being cramped did not bother them. Both were dead.

Wails rose up as people crowded close to help the wounded down. Helene got through to her father's side; he was dirty, unshaven, sunken-eyed and silent. The Luger pistol was still in its holster under his coat but there was no sign of the rifle. Trygve waved off the distraught questions people hurled at him and tiredly called for help getting the dead men out of his car.

Kasimir was there looking white as death as Eino Kurikka and Alexis Kanth helped his uncle away from the auto. Jannes Wilko and another man supported Franz Vasaanen towards the store where Hans moved aside for them to enter. The village, which had been quiet before, now seemed to spawn more people than the houses could have accommodated, and everyone was talking at once, some yelling, all hustling this way and that until a great scream arose down beside the dusty automobile where a woman had thrown herself upon one of the corpses. The scream tended to bring a little measure of quiet. It also put people's teeth on edge.

Marta was there. When Franz was eased into a chair her burly figure rudely forced a path and she sank down beside her husband. 'Whisky,' she said to Helene. Looking up at the four men standing glumly by, Marta singled out one. 'Someone must go for the doctor down at Raanujarvï. There must be others coming back. Someone must go quickly.'

One of the men turned without a word and walked out of the store. A second one followed him. Helene brought the whisky and Marta got several raw swallows down her husband. She then fell to examining the splinted leg. There was a dirty old bandage made of the trouser-leg. It was sticky with caked blood. Franz's hands were black, his clothing torn as though by brambles, his face mottled as much from fatigue as from shock and pain. Marta stood up, sent Helene for a wet cloth and said, 'Well; you had to go, didn't you?'

Franz gazed at her, at Hans Einhorst, and when Helene returned he also looked at her. The shock seemed less than it had before. He said, 'It is better than you think — except for one thing. We killed seven of them and captured four. We caught them so easily no one thought it possible.'

'Yes,' muttered Marta, her dread turning to such enormous relief she wished to castigate him. 'And how many more of you were hurt or killed?'

'None. Two killed, four wounded. Gunnar and I the most seriously injured. We had to come back but the others could go on.'

She washed his face, a trifle roughly to be true, but well. He made a grimace, looked round for the whisky and Helene handed him the bottle. He drank and passed it back, colour coming into his face. 'The wound isn't bad,' he told them, looking at the feverish leg. 'No bone was broken but some flesh was torn away. Painful but not very serious.'

'No,' scolded Marta, looking at the cumbersome, unclean bandage. 'No, it's not serious — unless you have gangrene from the dirt and they must remove the leg.'

Franz smiled a little. 'I'll be fit for the trip to Raanujarvï by tomorrow. More than anything else I need food and rest.' He looked at them all again, his gaze slowly fixing itself upon Hans as though a blow had fallen, but slowly, because his reflexes, mental as well as physical, were badly impaired by what he'd recently come through. 'Ahhhh,' he murmured. 'Helene . . . ?'

She stepped between her father and Einhorst. 'We'll get you home and into bed. Someone has already gone down to Raanujarvï for the doctor. Father; nothing else matters right now; do you understand? Nothing else matters.'

Franz could no longer see the face of the handsome youth and the whisky was busy inside his empty gut. He feebly struggled against sleep and apathy but the whisky won. He nodded, let his clouding gaze drop and Helene nodded at her mother. They would have tried it alone but Hans and the remaining villager moved in, got Franz between them and told the women to lead the way. They carried him from the door onward because at the door both his legs, the sound one and the splinted one, suddenly gave way.

Fortunately Franz and Marta had the downstairs bedroom, but even so it was a long walk and Franz Vasaanen was heavy. The men put him on to the bed and leaned a moment breathing heavily. Franz had passed out. Marta sniffed about that and went to the kitchen to make coffee. The villager left and Hans went back outside as though to also leave, but Helene caught him out there. She stood straight and grave when she thanked him for helping. He probed her expression, a faint scowl upon his brow.

'I want to talk to you,' he said. 'Why did your father look at me like that just before the liquor took over?'

Helene slid her gaze away, let it wander back down where the car stood, alone and deserted now, even the corpses having been taken away. 'He — was a little delirious.' She looked back. 'Hans; there won't be any time now for a few days. You'd probably better just go on.'

He really scowled now, both brows dropping into a wintery line above his eyes. 'I don't think so, Helene. I'm going to stay until we talk. If it takes a few days, I'll wait. Or a month; I'll still wait.'

She twisted as her mother called garrulously from inside. She said swiftly, 'All right. But we can't meet down by the hostel again.'

'Then where?'

'Well; behind the town where there are clearings and little pastures, the forest comes down. I'll meet you out there at sundown or a little after. Watch for me.'

He nodded and left. She went inside where Marta had the bandage off Franz's leg, the spruce splints tossed aside, and was cleansing the wound with water that had a smelly disinfectant in it. Without looking up her mother said, 'Helene; we'll need clean cloths and the bottles of salve in the chest.'

They worked with the leg for almost an hour, or until the better part of the afternoon was gone, then they got a little bitter black coffee down him. Helene left and Marta got him undressed and into bed. He was beginning to snore by then which indicated that what the whisky had initially accomplished, had now been taken over by the thorough exhaustion. He would sleep a long while, undoubtedly, and there was good reason to believe that when he awakened in the morning he'd have a mild headache.

Gunnar Mainpaa's injury, caused by a bullet bouncing off stone and grazing the side of his head, was even less serious than Franz's injury, so after bathing, shaving, eating a bigger meal than he'd eaten in years, he was willing to explain what had happened. He did this while sitting on a chair outside his store, which was next to the Vasaanen store where several dozen villagers were gathered, including Kasimir, who, although standing close to Hans Einhorst, did not see the youth at all; in fact never once turned his head in the direction of Einhorst.

'We were on the trail, which wasn't hard to see since they'd only very recently left the tracks from the Wilko farm and it hadn't rained. Eric said he didn't think we should follow the tracks, but should swing off to the left and make a big circle so that if they were up ahead somewhere and heard us coming, we wouldn't be ambushed.

'But we only did as Eric suggested for a short while then it became night. Some of the men had whisky. We drank a little. It had been a very strenuous day. Well; the next morning when we were preparing to go on, one of the men who had got up much earlier, came back to say that he could lead us right up to the edge of the camp where those brigands were. Eric said it was impossible; that the Germans couldn't be anywhere close. But we went — and we found them. . . . Well; two of us were killed and three or four wounded. Franz Vasaanen and I most seriously, and actually, except that it knocked me down and senseless for an hour or so, this graze is nothing. Anyway, you probably already know what we did to the Germans — killed seven outright and took some more prisoner who were lying so close they couldn't jump up and run when their friends ran. That was when we killed them. When they got desperate and sprang up to run. It was like shooting ducks in the marshes when they lift off the water.'

'Uncle,' put in Kasimir. 'Where are the others who went with you?'

'Well; they are still pursuing the Germans I suppose. They were all pleased at our success because we knew what you people who stayed in the village thought — a lot of old men rushing out to do something foolish.'

The facts were meagre and succinct, but they were also satisfactory — except for the two dead men from Joki. Trygve left to go back as soon as he'd eaten and rested a bit. Of course there must also be a pair of funerals, and as a few gloomy people predicted, more funerals later on.

Hans walked thoughtfully back down to the hostel where his bicycle and affects were. He went out to the river, found a secluded spot, stripped and bathed, shaved with the aid of a small steel mirror, washed a few things in the water and took them back to be hung up to dry.

He ate tinned rations without a qualm; since being on the tour that's just about all he ate, except of course for cafés in the larger towns. But he didn't object at all. In fact, Hans was not a big eater, ever, and right now he was even less of a one.

He was puzzled that the police or the Finnish army didn't hunt down those brigands. He was also a little sardonic about those outlaws being termed 'Germans' by everyone. He could understand why, of course, but he wondered nonetheless if there was a single German among them; if, in fact, they weren't simply brigands who'd come together and who now lived like Red Indians in the forest. Probably Russians, or Balkan renegades; possibly even Swedish or Finnish. He shrugged. It didn't matter to him who they were.

The sun was fast dropping. He started around through the village in order to be back by the trees when Helene came. He had other things to reflect upon instead of a few brigands in a remote Finnish village.

CHAPTER TEN

The Arrival Of Soldiers

She met him in the shadowless evening where tall trees stood making a black background, with the village down below them and visibly shining farther off, the river itself.

The forest, at least in this spot and for some little distance around, was upon a lift of slightly higher ground. There was something very old nearby that might have at one time been a stone tower, circular, roughly mortared, decayed now to little more than a jumble of lichen-covered stone. That's where he took her because they could sit there while they talked, the town below, the forest behind, and everywhere else, silence or the high heavens, or, a considerable distance westerly, the broad, steely river.

She told him the doctor had arrived. He nodded, having heard an automobile earlier. She also told him her father's leg seemed unlikely to give him serious trouble although the doctor said he might end up walking with a slight limp from now on; that being neither a young nor thin man, the injured muscles could not be expected to respond as well as they otherwise might.

He had little to say about that. She started to mention something else irrelevant and he stopped her, looking puzzled and hurt. She was different towards him; not cold, not particularly cool even, but different — as though she were obliged to tell him things about Joki, and the small skirmish somewhere behind them miles distant in the forest, like he were a cousin or a friend.

Whatever had happened, he knew, had only just occurred; since the previous night, when they'd been together down near the river. He asked about the men who'd slipped up on him. She knew nothing except that she thought they would gossip. He shrugged that off as being part of village life, world-wide. He said, 'Helene; suppose I didn't return to school. Suppose I stayed right here.'

She shot him a quick, strange glance. 'How could you do that, Hans; what would make you wish to do such a thing? There's nothing here for engineers. For fishermen, farmers, woodsmen, even storekeepers, yes. But what could an engineer do here — besides starve?'

That irritated him. 'Because a man has been educated to a trade,' he said shortly, 'doesn't mean he can't learn other things.' He started to say something more but checked himself, made a slow, critical study of her and gently shook his head. 'Why were you crying when you ran home last night, Helene?'

She stood up, considered the crumbled stonework, touched the rough mortar and slowly turned towards him. 'Women cry easily, Hans. It was — nothing very much.'

'And why don't you want me to stay in Joki?'

'I didn't say that.'

'You didn't have to. You meant it. That's the same thing.'

She stood in front of him watching the darkness of his mood mantle each changing expression. Anger made him no less handsome to her. She smiled and reached to touch him. 'Stay if you like,' she murmured.

'Well; would you like that, Helene?'

She continued to smile up at him. 'Hans; I'm thinking of your parents down in Essen. Of your one more year at college. Of the future that lies before you as an engineer.' She gestured. 'Look at this village. It is pleasant for older people. For younger ones too, of course, except that there's no future here unless one wants to work on the river, in the forests, in a little store for the rest of one's life.'

He didn't look at the village. He said, 'No one can make people stay where they don't want to stay, Helene. Next summer when I return we'll —'

'Listen,' she broke in swiftly. 'I hear a lorry down on the road.'

'The hell with a lorry,' he snapped, but she was turning away, looking down where it was possible to discern the road as it came up towards Joki. She pointed. It was a lorry all right and a quite large one at that. There was a drab, tan cover over the body. The vehicle stood nearly as tall as a man above the wheels. It travelled at a ponderous but undeviating speed straight into the village where it halted, a metal tailgate clanged down and men began climbing down. Moonlight shone off metal.

Hans said, sounding very disgruntled, 'It's your army arriving.'

She sounded relieved when she answered him. 'Now the men can come back home.'

'Is there some particular man you'd like to see come home, Helene?'

She turned, shocked, then, after staring at him a moment, she started briskly back down towards the village. As before, she left him standing. He seemed half of a mind to rush after her but he didn't do it. He sank back down upon the ancient stone, said something unpleasant in German and picked up a stone which he hurled into the forest where it echoed and re-echoed as it struck and bounced, then bounced again.

He knew he should leave Joki. He'd never been so ecstatic nor so plunged to the depths in a place before in his life. He would have left too, except that he did not intend to depart like this. Whatever it was that had turned her against him — if that's what it was — he wanted to know about.

He doubted that it was shame. At least not entirely, because whenever they met she looked him in the eye and didn't handle herself in a self-conscious manner. He wondered, finally, arising to stumble back down to the hostel, if his being German mightn't have something to do with it.

As ridiculous as this was, nevertheless he'd seen other perfectly rational people in Joki use the term 'German' as though it were synonymous with leprosy.

He'd been at the log hostel only a few minutes, hadn't had time to prepare for bed yet, when the soldiers came down there with their officer, a noncommissioned officer, and their lorry driver. The officer explained to Hans that he'd billet his men inside the log structure. Hans was perfectly agreeable; he didn't sleep indoors anyway, but always outside under the stars. He asked the officer — a captain — if he was here because of the fight between brigands and villagers. The captain was a lithe, pleasant, brisk young man, obviously from the big cities and also obviously not precisely delighted at this present duty. He said, 'Yes; but if they'd left those men alone I wouldn't be here now in the middle of the night.'

'There was some kind of raid,' said Hans. 'I've heard them discussing it.'

The captain sent his men under the noncommissioned officer into the log structure with orders for them to bed down. He then turned his full attention upon Hans. 'You are German, are you not?' he asked, speaking in that language.

Hans gave his name, a city of origin, and purpose for being in Finland, although he offered no explanation for being in Joki alone.

The captain lit a cigarette. 'A raid,' he said contemptuously. 'A farmer is forced to feed some starving beggars with guns.' He studied

Hans a moment then said, 'If you've heard this much you must also have heard that the raiders were Germans supposedly left over from the war.'

'I've heard them called Germans,' agreed Hans, 'although I don't know anything else about them. And I wonder if they really are Germans.'

'Of course not,' grumbled the captain. 'After a quarter of a century? People have to be soft in the head to think anything so ridiculous. Oh; there's probably a German or two among them, exactly as there may be a Serb, a Balt, a Montenegran — who knows what all? But Russians of course, and possibly a renegade Swede or two. Germans my foot!'

The captain yawned, stamped on his smoke and smiled. Hans smiled back not sure why he had to smile but doing so nonetheless. The officer looked round. Joki was alight up the distant roadway. A few people were abroad. The captain spoke again, less scornful this time.

'It is a pretty little place. Nothing a person would want to live in, but pretty, eh?'

Hans said it was indeed a pretty little village. Then he said, 'Captain; would you prohibit me from accompanying your party when you go into the forest after these brigands?'

The officer looked round swiftly. 'Of course I would prohibit it. You are a visitor to Finland. Think of the noises people would make if something happened to you.'

'Nothing is going to happen. I simply want to see for myself that these are Germans.'

'No need to go with us to discern that; just wait here a couple of days — a week at the most — until we return. We'll have some brigands for you to see.' The officer lifted a thick arm and waved it over the area indicating the farthest forest. 'There is a company of soldiers coming in from above. We will close in from below. East and west we'll have what you people used to call *jagers* on the flanks. The brigands won't stand a chance. And for my part I'm sick and tired of hearing of these men; I want to see them cleaned out once and for all. But as for you coming along, Herr Einhorst — *nein.* I can't assume the responsibility.'

'And if there were no responsibility, Captain? If I went along anyway?'

The captain smiled indulgently. In years he wasn't too much older than Hans, but obviously in all the ways that separated men from boys, he was much older and wiser and perhaps tougher. 'No. You stay here. Be a little patient. If there are Germans out there, believe me I'll bring you one back. Otherwise, I'd say you might as well brush up on Swedish and Russian.'

The captain went inside the log house, Hans stood a while in thought. After a bit, when all was quiet, he sat on his sleeping bag thinking. That was where the noncommissioned soldier found him when the older man came outdoors in his bare feet to study the sky, the village, the forest that blotted out so much and which blended with the blue-black sky. The man lustily cleared his throat and spat, then turned, regarded Hans a moment and sauntered over to say, 'I heard you and the captain talking in German. I myself only speak Finnish and English. Do you by any chance understand either?'

'English,' said Hans, studying the sergeant who was grey and hard-faced and obviously a professional in his line of endeavour.

'I see. But you are German, no?'

'Yes. From Essen.'

'A lot of steel mills there,' mused the sergeant, leaning upon the log wall and turning pensive. 'One time I had a very close friend from Essen. A soldier. A German soldier. You are too young to recall and probably no one ever told you: did you know thousands of Finnish soldiers marched into Russia with the Germans during the Second World War?'

Hans didn't know. He didn't care whether Finns and Germans had invaded Russia together. He would have liked to have got into his sleeping bag.

'So now the Germans are slipping about in the northern forests,' said the sergeant with a snort. 'Well; it was hard, back in those earlier times. A Finn didn't know from day to day who his friends or his enemies were. Finland declared war on Germany. That was a farce too. Many of us marched with the Germans and fought beside them. I tell you, young man, these times are a lot easier to understand. Except that the peasants always blame everything on Germans when the real enemy of Finland has always been Russia.'

The sergeant looked down. Hans was sitting with his back to the log building, his knees drawn up and both arms hooked round them. His appearance was that of a patient man waiting for something to end. The sergeant straightened up, said 'Good night,' and went heavily back around to the front of the building.

But Hans continued to sit for a long while after the loudest snore rose over the lesser snores inside, and when he finally did climb down into his sleeping bag he still wasn't tired.

The sky was flawless, the little late-night chill was coming, forest-fragrance lay everywhere, and except for the adenoidal rumblings coming from inside the hostel, there was peace and serenity everywhere but inside the heart of Hans Einhorst.

He didn't really care very much whether those brigands turned out to be Germans or not, but he had at least found an excuse for staying on, which he fully intended to do until he had it from Helene herself what it was that had come so abruptly between them.

He wanted to ask her to marry him; he had in fact meant to do that as soon as he dared, after returning, but the opportunity had never been exactly proper, and now it was beginning to appear that not only wouldn't the correct time come, but it seemed highly unlikely that she'd

agree even if he got up the nerve, and if the opportunity arose so that he might bring the subject up.

All he'd ever wanted was for her to help him
arrive at a means for re-ordering his upset life.
What else he wanted had never been the slightest
bit in doubt in his mind or his heart.

CHAPTER ELEVEN

A Startling Interlude

At five in the morning before anyone was stirring Trygve Vesainen drove into the village with four more wounded men. In contrast to their first encounter which had been so signally successful, these four men were the result of an ambush.

Only because the ambuscade had been accomplished in the dark, said the least injured of thc villagers, no one had been killed and the men with Eric Vendson had been able to beat back the brigands.

By six o'clock the captain had his soldiers on the move; neither he, his grizzled sergeant, nor any of their men were the least bit amiable as they struck out for the forest. The last thing the captain said was to Gunnar Mainpaa: 'You keep this student here; if you let him get away and he follows us I'm going to hold you directly responsible. If anything were to happen to him it could easily become a cause for trouble between Finland and Germany. And anyway, I don't want a civilian tagging along.'

Helene had stood aghast, staring at Hans. After Gunnar lectured the tall youth and went away with others to look after the injured, she took his arm and drew him into a doorway.

'Why would you want to go, Hans?'

'I just wanted to see whether or not they were Germans.'

'They would kill you. They've already killed two of our men.'

'Oh; no one's going to kill me. I simply wanted —'

'Hans! Promise me you won't go after the soldiers. Promise me!'

He felt her nails bite into his arm. It was delicious pain. He touched her cheek. It was warm and velvety. 'I love you very much, Helene. I don't believe it's possible for one person to love another any more.'

Tears sprang into her eyes. They were visible even in the moonless, sunless, pre-dawn. She went in closer, let him close his arms around her and placed her cheek upon his chest. They stood like that for perhaps ten seconds before the scuff of someone walking down towards them made her tear free and turn.

It was Kasimir. 'The doctor has those wounded men at your house. Your mother sent me to find you. She needs more help up there.'

'Yes, Kasimir. Thank you for telling me. I'll go right along.'

The hunchback didn't offer to depart. He looked from Helene to Hans and back again. Finally he said, 'I see that it was all a mistake, the other night. That fool of a Jannes Wilko.' Kasimir then angrily stalked away across the road and southward towards his home.

Hans was exasperated. For a moment she'd

melted towards him the way she'd done before he'd ever left the village. Then that crab-walking cripple had to interrupt. He glared after Kasimir until Helene said, 'Did you promise you wouldn't follow the soldiers, Hans?'

'No. But I will promise you, providing you'll let me help you with the wounded.'

Her answer shot back so suddenly and harshly he was startled by it. 'No! You can't do that! my father wouldn't understand.' She turned and started away, but this time his patience was thinned down by irritation so he ran over, caught her roughly and spun her back facing him. She was startled by his expression; by the pale flame in his eyes and the cruel lines around his mouth.

'The hell with what your father understands and doesn't understand,' he snarled, holding her so tightly she bit her lip against the pain. 'I've had enough of this — now you tell me what has happened; why you cry one minute, stay close to me the next minute, and then want me to go away in such a big hurry. I want to know, Helene. I *mean* to know!'

'You are hurting my arms,' she said past clenched teeth. When he loosened his hold, then dropped his hands entirely, she waited a moment, giving him that much time for the quick, hot anger to pass, then she said, 'With us it was sudden love, Hans. I didn't know it could happen like that.'

'All right, Helene, but it *did* happen like that. And it's still happening, at least on my side. If you've changed tell me. Tell me what I've done. What I must do to put things as they were. Tell me!'

'Hans, I have to go help my mother with the injured men. If you're out front after sundown I'll go for a walk with you. I'll — tell you. Is that all right?'

'Yes, I suppose it will have to be.' He loosened a little, his voice losing its edge. 'I'm sorry, Helene.' I didn't mean to hurt you. But this is a hard time for me. You have no idea how hard a time.'

'I have an idea, Hans,' she said simply. 'To-night.'

He let her go, watched a bit, then with fisted hands sunk in trouser pockets he started walking back down where Trygve Vesainen's filthy automobile stood. Eino Kurikka was standing with both hands behind his back gazing at the auto. Eino had a stub of a smoke between his lips. He looked over, recognized Hans and said, as though there's never been any unpleasantness between them, 'Look. Isn't that a bullet hole in the door of the car?'

Hans thought it was but then he'd never before seen a bullet hole in an automobile. Eino opened the door; on the inside the hole was more ragged. Eino seemed pleased or proud. He said he guessed those infernal Germans had learned Finns were good forest-fighters too.

Hans got clear and resumed his way. Back at the hostel he considered the amount of time he had to kill. He also turned somewhat annoyed by this constant meeting. It would be bad enough in broad daylight — as though they were small children full of giggles and embarrassment — but at night, skulking here and there like fugitives, was prolonging an initial tentativeness a good deal longer than was necessary.

He felt resentment towards the villagers too, whose sole interest was this asinine little mini-war in a vast and shadowy forest. Several had been wounded and the village acted as though a national calamity had occurred.

And her father; she'd said he'd be upset at sight of Hans. Undoubtedly he was one of those old devils who classified all evil as 'German'.

The longer he sat thinking the more odds appeared to pile up against him — against *them*. Had he been a less resolute, persevering individual, he just might have got on to his bicycle and gone down the road as Helene had suggested.

That idea did not now occur to him, but another idea did appear; as soon as Helene's father was decently able to have visitors he'd go see him. Of course he'd speak of his love for Helene but that would be only a part of what he'd say to the old man.

He sat a while organizing his thoughts, forming them into words, and arranging the subjects in a kind of relevant sequence so that when he spoke to Helene's father he'd sound very rational.

A sound caught his attention, scattering thoughts and bringing his head around. A tall, raw-boned older man was viewing him round the edge of the log building. The older man had a revolver shoved into his belt and looked white around the lips, looked stricken and ready to drop. Hans was too startled by the man's look to do more than nod.

The big man muttered something Hans didn't understand. In reply, Hans used German. At once the older man's big, unshorn head lifted, his light eyes fell with something akin to hope brightening them. In the same tongue the large man said, 'I have been injured, young man. You must help me.' He opened his jacket to disclose a soggy, torn segment of shirt beneath and a patch of dirty skin with a purplish, puckered wound. There was something suspiciously similar between the swollen hole in the man's side and the hole in the door of the automobile belonging to Trygve Vesainen.

Hans came upright in one lithe movement. 'There's a *doktor* in the village,' he said. 'Come; I'll take you to him.'

'*Nein!* I cannot go there. Come with me; lend me your shoulder. I'll show you a place. Come, come!'

The older man's weathered, harsh face was insistent without being the least bit menacing. Although the revolver showed plainly he seemed not the least bit aware of possessing the weapon. He looked ready to collapse. Hans moved to

109

assist him even though he was just beginning to have some unpleasant suspicions about this big stranger who spoke un-accented German.

The older man moved automatically, lifting and dropping each foot. He did not really need Hans's shoulder until they began going up the mild incline of the hillock behind town, then, if he'd have rested as Hans suggested, he would have made the climb without help. But he wouldn't rest. The large vein in the side of his neck throbbed powerfully. Once, when he stopped to open the jacket and look, Hans saw the blood running from the wound; it made him a little queasy.

The big man knew the forest; knew every tree it seemed, for he'd mutter directions and look annoyed when Hans would try to lead him in a direction different from the one he preferred. Also, he seemed to lose a good deal of the urgency which had showed down in the village as they progressed.

Hans stopped near a downed, dead tree, eased his charge into a sitting position and when the older man complained about stopping saying he wasn't tired, and moreover it was only a little further along, Hans said, 'I wasn't thinking of you; it is I who am exhausted.'

The older man raised his shaggy head slowly turning it left and right, listening, then he dropped it down again, staring at the ground, lips twisted in thin bitterness.

Hans reflected. He was certain his companion

was some wounded brigand. The fact that the man was obviously German made Hans wonder if, after all, the villagers weren't correct while he and the army captain had been wrong. Of course one injured brigand didn't mean all brigands were Germans.

They went on, but now the larger and heavier man's weight was becoming an increasing burden. They came through a veil of new-growth spruce, small and sturdy and bushy, bluish rather than green, and emerged into a small, neat and grassy clearing where a log house stood. The injured man's strength seemed to dwindle faster at sight of the little house. In fact Hans scarcely got him inside past the open door before he collapsed entirely. Hans used the last of his own depleted strength to half lift, half push, the big man on to a bunk-bed made against one windowless wall.

He sat on a chair to rest legs and lungs with perspiration running under his shirt and trousers. He was vague about the directions he'd followed reaching this place but he was even more vague about the stranger and why he'd come to Hans, if indeed he hadn't just been searching for anyone in his desperate condition.

After a bit Hans arose, explored the cabin, which only possessed two rooms and one of those, the smaller, seemed to have been added on the back of the larger room some time after the house had originally been constructed.

There was nothing much to be viewed; an iron

stove, cooking utensils, several old guns in corners, a metal-bound box which once had been the property of someone whose name had been nearly obliterated by an application of hot irons to the front, where the hasp and lock were, along with some home-made chairs, benches, tables, and of course the bunk where the unconscious man lay moaning. There were shelves and even a built-in cupboard in the kitchen, or smaller, lean-to room. From these Hans procured clean cloths for bandaging. From a barrel near the rear door he got clean water in a saucepan. Then he returned to the bed, lay open the man's jacket, put the pistol aside, soaked the fragments of shirting loose from the clotted wound, and went to work.

He knew very little of first-aid but in this case obviously the wound had to be cleansed so he set about doing that. He stopped only when he'd made an examination and discovered that while the bullet had struck the man in the side, it had not simply torn flesh but had burrowed inward as well — and had not emerged because there was no exit-hole in back.

The bleeding seemed to occur only when the man moved. Now, there was a bare trickle. Hans had no difficulty staunching that. He then made a wet compress, placed it over the injury, put a dry one atop it, and encircled the man's body with strips of cloth to hold the compresses in place. Beyond that he could do nothing. As he rinsed both hands before leaving the cabin he decided to go directly to the Vasaanen's house where the doctor had been when last he'd heard, and bring the practitioner back here, even though, as soon as he stepped through the door and saw the gloom settling throughout the forest, he wasn't quite sure he'd know the way back.

He *did* know the general direction though, and struck out due westward. He hadn't actually gone deep enough into the forest to be lost in any case. But by the time he saw the lights, the distant river, the ugly black blocks which were houses and stores, it was dark out.

CHAPTER TWELVE

The Swede Who Is Not A Swede

Helene was standing in the silver night wearing a sweater. She saw him coming, not from the direction she'd been watching, and turned to walk forward.

'I thought you'd be coming from down by the hostel,' she said, looking at him. Then she stopped speaking, stopped moving, and said, 'What's the matter, Hans?'

'What *isn't* the matter,' he muttered, taking her arm and starting along northwards, away from her home and the more southerly centre of Joki. 'Helene; I was down at the hostel. A man came along asking for help. He'd been hurt — shot in the body. I —'

'Shot?' She stopped dead still.

He didn't repeat it. 'He needs a doctor. From the looks of him I think he needs the doctor very badly.'

'Hans; where is he?'

'There's a little cabin up in the forest in a small clearing. I took him there. Helene; I cleansed the wound and bandaged him, but I think the bullet must still be inside him. I've heard that causes blood-poisoning.'

'The doctor is spending the night with us, Hans. I'll go back and —'

'Wait. There's something else. I think this man is one of the brigands. He is German, at least, and he was wearing a pistol, and obviously, he's been in a fight.'

Helene listened to each swift-spoken word without moving. Eventually she said, 'Hans; why would he come to you?'

'Why? How would I know why? I was simply sitting in the shade on the far side of the hostel and looked round at a noise, and there he was. Maybe he thought that by reaching the edge of the village he might catch a ride down towards Raanujarvï.'

Helene twisted slowly from the waist to run a thoughtful glance back down towards the centre of the village as she said, 'A German brigand. Hans, you've helped one of the German brigands.'

'Damn it, I'd probably have helped him if he'd been an Armenian or even a Frenchman. What's that got to do . . . ?' He let it trail off into long silence while they looked at one another.

She nodded. 'You know what everyone will think if they discover what you've done. Hans, you are also a German.'

He twisted his face into an expression of exasperated annoyance. 'No one can be that biased, can they?'

'In Joki they can, Hans. And they will.'

He stepped to a fence in front of a lighted house and leaned upon it. 'I feel strangled by something — by ignorance, by unreasoning bias.

Good God, the war was a lifetime ago, and anyway you Finns fought *with* the Nazis more than against them.' He threw up his hands. 'Good Lord, there must be some place in the world where people aren't chock-full of all these poisonous inhibitions and ancient animosities. America perhaps.'

'You wouldn't think so if you were black-skinned in America, Hans. Anyway, what's to be done about your wounded man?'

'Why, take the doctor to him. What else? I surely can't remove that bullet.'

She turned thoughtful again. 'If we take him up there and he afterwards talks. . . .'

'You mean your villagers would kill an injured man, Helene?'

'Have you seen the kinsmen of those two dead villagers since the bodies were brought back; or their friends, or any of the other angry people who've had their fathers and brothers wounded? They could kill your German in his bed!'

Hans shook his head. 'Helene; the man is going to die up there in the forest. That bullet will poison him. He'll probably be a week swelling up, turning purple, moaning and tossing, and in the end he'll die. Which is better — to leave him alone to die in prolonged agony, or take the doctor to him and take a chance on the villagers not finding out, not killing him in his delirium?'

She didn't answer.

He straightened up off the board fence. 'In his

116

shoes I'd prefer a bullet now. Anyway, isn't it possible the doctor would keep his mouth closed?'

She shrugged. 'That's not the point. Even if the doctor doesn't say anything someone is going to see you going up there and get curious. Or else they'll . . . Where is this cabin where you hid him?'

'A mile or more east, I think, and slightly northward back in the trees. Do you know it?'

She nodded. She'd been up there a few times with others, but only as a child and it had been a long time ago. But that wasn't important right at this juncture so she said, 'I'll go back and get the doctor. I'll have to get him out of the house without rousing my parents. You come back with me and wait. I'll have to lie, I suppose.' She looked him squarely in the eye. 'I've learned to do that, lately,' she said, sounding bitter. He caught some innuendo but didn't dwell on it right at the time because she turned, taking his arm and starting back.

She was very practical now, telling him that everyone at her house was exhausted; it had been a long day what with caring for the wounded and afterwards seeing them off in the company of friends and relatives. Also, her father'd awakened in the morning feeling vastly recuperated everywhere except in the head. Moreover, the doctor hadn't had a moment's rest, because now that he was in Joki, everyone who'd had a complaint of any kind since his previous visit in early springtime, came round to the Vasaanen home to discuss ailments with him.

Her mother and father, she was reasonably certain, were abed and fast asleep, for while it was still quite early they were not young nor inured to the variety of stress under which they'd been labouring lately. The physician too would be asleep, she was sure, but since he had her own upstairs bedroom while he was a guest, she was confident of being able to rouse him without also rousing her parents.

She left Hans at the front gate feeling more than ever like a culprit or fugitive, and hastened into the house. He stood in shadows watching a couple strolling along farther down nearer the centre of the village. He jumped when a man's voice, sounding irritable, called a dog somewhere among the opposite houses.

He began to wish he'd refused to help that wounded man. All the implications of his gallantry hadn't occurred to him until after he'd listened to Helene's reaction and her conviction of what the reaction would be throughout her village, if people learned of his predicament.

He had, he finally decided, come to Finland, at least to this part of Finland, at perhaps the worst possible time. But he shrugged that off; he was here and that alone mattered right at this moment. How he would afterwards extricate himself he had no idea. Nor did he more than passingly reflect upon the original purpose of his meeting tonight with Helene. She'd been going to tell him what was troubling her. Perhaps she still would, but right now, hearing sounds up near the front of the Vasaanen house, it didn't seem very important.

Helene had a thickly-made, grey, average-sized older man walking down towards him, at her side. The man had a worn old leather bag in one hand and although he was wearing a jacket, he had no tie on.

Helene introduced them outside the front gate. 'Doctor; this is Hans Einhorst, the man who found the wounded person. Hans; this is Doctor Leino.'

The physician bent a keen glance upon Hans as they gripped hands. He seemed about to ask a question, then changed his mind and motioned. 'I don't appreciate these late calls but since I'm committed, let us get on with it.'

Hans led out but twice Helene corrected his directions through the rear environs of the village, in a part he was not familiar with. By the time they reached the utter silence and blackness of the forest Hans had to stop to get back his bearings. Helene was impatient and pointed the way. She possessed that most typical Finnish instinct: a perfect sense of direction even without points of reference, no small matter in a night-darkened forest where every tree looked like every other tree.

Doctor Leino looked dour but he did not complain. However, when they came to the downed old dead tree where Hans had rested earlier with his companion, the doctor heaved a great sigh as he sank down looking round. 'Unpleasant place,' he said. 'On a night like this it's not hard to understand how people used to imagine all manner of frightful creatures, blood-sucking and otherwise, inhabited forests. Eh?'

They went on, Helene no longer quite as sure as before but Hans taking over now and unerringly following his former path until they came within sight of the moon-softened clearing and the yonder cabin. 'Here,' Doctor Leino grunted. 'A setting for one of the old German fables, eh, *Herr* Einhorst?'

Hans looked back. Among these people, even under adverse circumstances, they would not let him forget that they considered him a German first, a human being second. He didn't answer the doctor.

They crossed the clearing and paused outside. Here, the silence was deeper than ever; despite themselves they bunched up a little. Hans stepped over, pushed inward on the door and passed from sight in the total blackness within. A moment later he had a candle burning. Helene and the physician then also entered. Hans found and lit three more candles, which seemed to give ample light for Doctor Leino, who set aside his battered old scuffed valise, crossed to the bed and bent slightly from the waist without touching the feverish man lying there.

After a bit he said, '*Herr* Einhorst, you were quite right. The bullet is still inside him. Of course it must come out, but then I can hardly undertake such an operation by candlelight, can I?'

Helene, moving closer with a candle in one hand, abruptly stopped, leaned and put the candle closer to the sweat-shiny, grey-slack face of the unconscious man. 'Eric,' she whispered. 'It's Eric Vendson. I didn't think . . . when you said he was a German, Hans, I didn't think it could be Eric, although the cabin you described was his.' She looked at Hans. 'You were mistaken. Eric is a Swede.'

Hans, watching the doctor's hands, probing now, peeling away the bandage he'd made, said nothing. It wasn't important whether the wounded man was German or Swedish.

But Helene repeated it, so Hans turned and said, 'Helene; I know a Swede when I hear one. This man is not a Swede. He is a German.'

Doctor Leino interrupted their argument by sending Helene out back to the lean-to for fresh water in a pan, and asked Hans to help him turn the injured man on to his side while he tried to trace the trajectory of the bullet and decide where it must be lodged.

Eric's body was hot to the touch and the physician made a little disapproving clucking sound about that. By the time Helene returned with the water — into which the physician promptly dipped his hands — Hans had eased Eric on to his back again. That disturbance seemed to jostle Eric's brain. He said in perfect German:

'There is no home left to go to, so we will make homes here.'

Doctor Leino turned to Helene. '*Herr* Einhorst is correct; this man is no Swede, he is German.'

Helene stared. 'But — he's always been the one who wanted to hunt down the brigands, saying they were Germans whom he despised for what they did in Sweden during the war. I've even heard Gunnar Mainpaa say hating Germans is a mania with Eric.'

Doctor Leino shrugged about that. 'Who knows what is inside another man's brain? Maybe he does hate Germans, I don't know — But I *do* know he is no Swede. Now suppose we arrange the candles better so that I can see, because we're going to have to go digging for the bullet. He is far too big for us to carry back to the village and the lead must come out.'

Hans was perspiring. He fixed the candles and brought over the doctor's old valise. Helene looked pale and nothing had happened yet, unless it was the sight of those clotted rags lying on the floor, the bandaging Hans had improvized, that made her look like that.

Hans said, 'Go into the other room, Helene; see if there is tea or coffee or something. We could all use some.'

She turned away and Doctor Leino smiled and winked at Hans. 'Better just one patient at a time, eh? Well; if she faints at least by the time she recovers we should be through.' He straightened up, removed his jacket, rolled up both sleeves to disclose powerful, hairy arms, dipped his hands into the water again then said, 'Between the two of us, *Herr* Einhorst, this man will die with the bullet in his belly or out of it. There is already too much poisoning, I'm afraid. Odd how fast it spreads in some and how slowly in others. Well; come over here — you can help steady him.'

Hans went over but he looked almost as white as Helene had looked. He locked his jaw and did not look at Doctor Leino at all, not even when he was given a brusque order.

CHAPTER THIRTEEN

Doctor Leino

It took ages to locate the pellet and ages more for the methodical, spatulate hands of Doctor Leino to lift it out, drop it with a 'clink' into the basin of pink water, and stop to wipe his face, look round at Hans, then bend close for a study of the eyes of his patient.

'The man co-operated very well,' he muttered. 'I was fearful he'd move at the wrong time. The bullet was deep.'

'Did it do much damage?' asked Hans.

Doctor Leino was honest. 'Enough. It did enough damage. Do you know — this man probably walked miles with that thing in him. In itself, it was no great feat, but with the torn and ripped entrails, every step must have been torture. The bullet must have come from a fair distance, though; I've seen many bullet wounds in my lifetime. As a rule, if they are fired up close, they make a disgusting mess of a man's belly and entrails. But from a distance they tend to go in clean and . . . What's the matter with you, young man? Well, well; excuse me. Go see if the young lady has the tea made, or coffee, or whatever it is.'

Hans got to the door with his back to Doctor Leino, to the gory belly of Eric, to the hideous shadows twice life-size, dancing every time a candle flickered, and hung there. Helene, kneeling on the far side of the room, arose without looking directly at Hans, went to the stove and lifted off a pot of coffee which smelled delicious although she said, speaking very low, that she'd been unable to find fresh grounds so she'd simply re-boiled what was already in the pot.

It didn't matter. Hans had no taste for coffee or anything else right then. He suggested, however, that she take a cup to Doctor Leino, then he dropped on to a chair at the kitchen table. She didn't obey; in fact she stood there watching Hans's head as it turned to the place where she'd been kneeling. She'd broken open the old metal-bounder box with the name burned off it. He had just enough light to make out several things: a black coat with white piping and metal insignias on each lapel. A uniform cap, also dark with white facing. A small satin-lined box holding a Knight's Cross. As he arose, moved over and picked up the box he knew exactly what would be in the centre of that Iron Cross — a small swastika. He was correct.

He turned and saw Helene watching. He put the box atop the table, bent and lifted the black uniform coat. Beneath it, neatly folded, were trousers to match, black boots, a handsome little embossed dagger with what appeared to be an ivory handle, and atop that handle was another of those small swastikas.

'SS, Helene,' he muttered, holding the dagger and coat. 'Your Swede was an SS man.' He dropped the coat but kept the dagger. 'Now what would your villagers do, if they came up here?'

She'd evidently already thought of that. Also, she knew what those emblems meant. 'They'd be as stunned as I was, Hans. Then they would kill him.'

He tossed the dagger back into the metal-bound box atop the uniform. There were several books too, and a string-held bundle of letters and papers. Hans shook his head. 'It's like opening a coffin,' he said, 'and smelling ancient dust.'

'But it doesn't make sense, Hans.'

He contradicted her. 'It makes sense enough. You heard what he said about there being no homes. He meant Germany after the war. So, I suppose your people were right after all. I think originally at any rate, those brigands in the forests *were* Germans. But after a quarter of a century there couldn't be very many left. Perhaps just Eric. And all his talk of hating Germans and hunting them down — I don't think so, Helene; I think he spied for them, kept them informed.'

'He led our men.'

'You heard your father say Eric didn't believe it when one of the villagers found the Germans. You also heard how the village men were ambushed this last time. Well; just imagine Eric *was* a brigand, then those other things make sense.'

126

Doctor Leino came into the doorway. He saw the opened box at once, strolled around, held a candle low then made a soft whistle. 'So you see,' he said, looking at Helene, 'our big friend in there actually was more than just a German — he was an SS man, the most despicable of all Germans.' Leino gazed at the Knight's Cross in its little velvet box and straightened up. 'I should have known this before. He could have laid in there and taken a month to die!'

Helene shivered, turned and poured three cups of powerful coffee, put them on the table and re-set the pot on the stove which was merrily crackling having been stoked with pitchy wood that made the cabin warmer than it otherwise could have been because by now it was quite chilly out. 'Please,' she said to Doctor Leino and Hans.

They sat, Doctor Leino's grizzled, lined face made faun-like in the eerie candlelight, Hans, solemn and tired-looking. Leino raised his cup. 'To our patient in the next room,' he rasped, 'who could not stop betraying his friends even so late in life.'

Hans didn't touch the cup in front of him. His strong, handsome features hardened towards the medical man. 'Just let him die,' he growled. 'It can't have been pleasant for him.'

'Pleasant?' said Doctor Leino. 'Of course it was pleasant for him — right up until someone put a bullet in his belly. Probably one of the villagers he was leading who may have seen that he'd let them all be ambushed. Pleasant, my young friend, is what you make of something. Don't pity that man in there, despise him.'

'I pity him,' Hans said, and sipped the bitter coffee. 'He doesn't need me to despise him, with everyone else on earth doing it so competently.'

'No, of course not,' said the burly doctor, looking straight at Hans. 'But then of course you are German.'

Helene recoiled as Hans half shot to his feet, hung there, then slowly eased back down again. 'You too, Doctor; you too . . . ?'

Leino's eyes wavered, fell to the cup of coffee and remained there. 'No. Not really, son.' He jerked his head to indicate the man in the next room. 'You have had proof tonight that the passage of time doesn't really change people very much. That man in there — he still remembered. I — of the same generation and with some tales of my own that I could tell you — I still remember.'

'And hate, Doctor?'

'Yes. I still hate from time to time. Like seeing that Iron Cross, that black suit and hat. The dagger.' Doctor Leino fished out a limp handkerchief, looked round, mopped his face and made a visible effort to lighten his mood. 'Bad enough, this poor light that makes us all resemble gargoyles, but bringing in all the things that died so long ago only makes it worse. You two are young. Well; you have my own best hopes and prayers — although I've never been much for prayers. Young lady; step to the door and see if our SS friend is still asleep.'

Helene stepped over, stood a moment, then Hans sprang up as she began to weave. He caught her as she fell and Doctor Leino, moving swiftly but not nearly swiftly enough, came to his feet too.

'Fainted,' he said, eyeing the quiet, lovely face cradled in Hans's arms. 'She should have fainted an hour ago. Not now; now it is all over. Well; I'll get some blankets and make her comfortable here on the floor. There is no other place with the German using the only bed.'

Hans lay Helene down very gently and kissed her before Doctor Leino returned dragging blankets — one of which was sticky with drying blood at the corner. As the medical man knelt he said, 'Go see if the patient is still bleeding, will you, *Herr* Einhorst?'

Hans went into the other room and while he was away Helene opened her eyes as Doctor Leino was punching up a pillow out of blankets. He sat back and gazed at her with a slightly sceptical expression. In a very low voice he said, 'Young lady, the time to have fainted was an hour ago. And even now, when you did faint, there was nothing very terrible to see.'

'I was — just tired,' murmured Helene, struggling to sit up.

Leino put a firm hand on her shoulder and held her down. 'You're not going anywhere for a moment. Just lie still.' His eyes were still sceptical. 'It wasn't the SS man that made you faint anyway.'

Helene's glance jumped to Doctor Leino's face. 'What do you mean?' she whispered.

'You must know what I mean,' he said, and held her wrist for the pulse-beat. 'Is it such a secret, then?'

She tried to arise again. He shook his head at her and smiled slightly. He put down the wrist, patted her and said, 'All right; then it *is* a secret, except that now I also know.' He thought on that, then added something to it. 'Of course in time everyone will know, but even before it becomes so obvious, if you are one of those women who faint, get sick to their stomachs, don't eat and mope around, it won't take the observant women of your village very long to suspect your secret.'

She clutched his sleeve, sat up and looked out into the other room. The only concession she made to Doctor Leino's inadvertent discovery was to say swiftly, as the sound of Hans returning reached them. '*He* must not know.'

Leino watched her beautiful face a moment, then got heavily to his feet, offered his hand and gently hauled her up too. He put her in a chair and scooped up the blanket with the scarlet corner and flung it over atop the box holding those Nazi mementoes. When Hans appeared he said, 'It's been quite a night for her.' Then Leino pointed at the coffee pot. 'Suppose we all have

130

one more drink of that stuff, then start back to the village.'

Hans went to Helene and laid a hand lightly upon her shoulder. She looked up, then down again. The physician had to re-fill their cups. There was just barely enough. He also rummaged the cupboards for whisky and desisted only when Hans asked a question.

'Do we leave Eric here, Doctor?'

'What else?' asked Leino, returning to the table. 'He's dead weight. We three couldn't get him down to the village. Anyway, all's been done for him that could be done even in the hospital down at Raanujarvï. Frankly, the man's chance is very slight. I think, in his place, I'd just as soon die right in my own bed. Moreover, supposing he were to recover. . . .' The physician looked meaningfully towards the metal-bound box.

Helene drank a little of her coffee. Hans sat down beside her and Doctor Leino, eyeing them both, was silent.

The candles were guttering in their dishes. One had already burnt out. No one had made any search for a replacement.

A rustling sound as of wind working through the hushed and menacing forest outside, scrabbled around a corner of the cabin. Helene shivered and reached for another drink from her cup.

'I don't understand,' she murmured. 'He was living a lie all these years.'

Both men understood to whom she referred but neither said anything. There really wasn't very much to be said once the double-life of Eric Vendson was revealed. The details would come out as time passed, naturally, but the real enigma of the man might never be fully understood. Still, it was enough to know that he'd been one of the brigands; had tried to lead the villagers into an ambush, had failed both sides and had been rewarded for his duplicity by a bullet.

Doctor Leino arose, said, "I suppose we can find our way back; we'd better start out now.' Then, looking at Hans, he also said, 'Perhaps it would be better if nothing were said about our SS man for a bit. Let me call down to Raanujarvï for the police first. We don't want something awkward to happen, do we?'

Hans helped Helene to her feet. She was all right now and moved away from his touch. He watched her with a perplexed expression.

In the larger room they were all drawn to the bed. Vendson — or whatever his name really was — lay like stone, his chest rising and falling shallowly, his face flushed. Doctor Leino was impersonal as he made a final check of the wound. 'Even penicillin or sulfa couldn't do much now. He must have carried that bullet in him for something like twenty-four hours.'

That little rustling sound came again as though there was a chill wind outside. Hans said perhaps they should devise some way to prevent Eric from tossing about and falling from the bed. Doctor Leino was indifferent to the suggestion saying he doubted very much if the man would fall out. He then went to the door and opened it as though to step through, stopped still in his tracks without a sound.

Hans and Helene, moving forward, saw the gun barrel without seeing who was holding it. The barrel was within six inches of Doctor Leino's stomach and holding steady.

CHAPTER FOURTEEN

The Way Back

The grizzled sergeant stepped inside pushing back Doctor Leino with a stiff arm. Three soldiers also entered the cabin. The sergeant saw Hans and Helene, stared briefly, then turned towards the sound of a low moan. His men closed the door and kept their rifles on their captives.

The sergeant went slowly over and peered into the face of Eric Vendson. He picked up a candle-holder and pushed it close as though wishing to make doubly certain who was moaning. Finally, still without a word being spoken, he set the candle back on the table, turned and studied his prisoners. He knew Doctor Leino for he said, 'Well; you appear to have saved him — for what?'

The answer was unruffled. 'For whatever will be done with him; what would you have done? Don't tell me, Sergeant. I know what you'd have done to him.'

The sergeant said something in Finnish to one of the soldiers. The man at once left the cabin. The two remaining men lowered their rifles and stood in front of the door. The second candle burned low and finally died altogether. It was grotesque now, for every human movement became exaggerated upon rough log walls, every face became a round, pale blob with indistinct features.

Doctor Leino asked a question: 'Who shot him; you or the others?'

'The others,' exclaimed the sergeant, casting another look at the feverish face on the bed. 'But we would have, if we'd have seen him.'

'What happened?'

'They caught on to what he was doing after they'd been ambushed. He tried to lead them away from the brigands. That might have gone unnoticed but he also set them up for an ambush. Even then, as they told us when we ran up after hearing the gunfire, they didn't believe he had done anything deliberately. But then the old fool made a real mistake — he let one of their captives escape with a message for the brigands to flee westward. The captain himself shot that one; the man told him how he'd escaped and what he was to tell the others. We were going after him when one of the villagers who'd seen Vendson release the prisoner, shot him. But you'll have to give the devil credit — he got all the way back here with my squad on his heels.' The sergeant paused, took a chair then said, 'Of course we saw enough blood to know we'd eventually find him, but to me it seemed insane for him to return here when he must have known we were after him.'

Helene said quietly, 'Go look in the metal-bound box in the other room, Sergeant. I think you'll find the reason why he returned. But he

135

collapsed before he could destroy anything.'

The sergeant looked towards the rearward doorway but made no move off his chair. Doctor Leino said, 'SS uniform and an Iron Cross, Sergeant.'

The soldier who'd been ordered out of the cottage returned about then, leading four more soldiers and the saturnine captain. These men also had two dishevelled, wan captives whom they roughly pushed inside the room. The captain saw Hans at once and looked wry about his presence away from the village but he said nothing as the sergeant arose and beckoned. He and the officer stepped into the lean-to section leaving everyone else in the outer room. One soldier took a torch from his belt, flicked it on and set it on the table. This brightness brought things back into proper perspective.

Hans got Helene a chair. Doctor Leino asked one of the soldiers if he had a cigarette; he did have and he also held a light for the physician. Only the two lean prisoners seemed stiff and tense. The soldiers gazed at Eric, lying still and silent now. They kept the door guarded until the officers returned from the back room.

Without a word the captain went to stand beside the bed gazing at the unconscious man. He stood with both hands in his pockets for quite a while, studying the feverish face. There was little of the sardonic, rough attitude of the sergeant. The captain, younger and with little to base animosity upon except stories, seemed to view the German as more a curiosity than a peril. He asked Doctor Leino whether the man would live or not. The answer he got was emphatic. 'No. Even with better facilities; he has been poisoned too long.'

The captain turned, gazed at Hans and said, 'I thought you were to remain in the village.'

'I found that wounded man and brought him here. He wanted to come here. Then I went after help.'

The captain shrugged and looked dispassionately at the prisoners. 'There are your Germans,' he said. 'We mopped up what the villagers hadn't already taken care of. A few, perhaps three or four, escaped, but the other troops will catch them. Take a good look; do they appear German to you people?' No one answered. It Would have been impossible to tell about either man without hearing them speak or hearing what they might say.

'Russians,' said the captain, using that same dispassionate tone. 'Your friend there on the bed was the only German except for another older man who was killed. The others were mongrels — Swedes, Russians, Hungarians.'

Hans asked one question: 'Is it true that originally there were more Germans?'

'Yes, it is true. But for the villagers to continue calling them Germans was foolish. I thought as much the time you and I discussed this before. Well; they won't bother anyone again. If others slip in to take their place, at least they won't have a spy in Joki to tell them where and when to raid.'

Doctor Leino finished his cigarette, stepped upon it and said, 'Captain; I had a hard day yesterday. Probably, it will be equally as hard tomorrow.'

'Yes of course,' replied the officer with a little smile at Doctor Leino. 'We'll go on down to the village. The others will probably arrive there in the morning anyway. There will be some wounded for you to care for.' He signalled for the door to be opened by the men guarding it. At once the sergeant moved in closer to the prisoners. He said in a chilly tone that the forest at night was an ideal place for fugitives and captives to try to hide. Then he laughed nastily and shoved the captives outside where his men, rifles ready, watched them move ahead.

One soldier was left behind. He didn't dispute the order but his expression showed that he was far from pleased with the assignment. They left him the electric torch for by this time the last of the stubby little candles had died out altogether.

The night was cold, the hour late, the forest more unpleasant than ever in spite of their increased numbers and their weapons. Hans walked with Helene while the sergeant stayed up front with the enlisted men, and the captain and doctor strolled together in quiet conversation. Helene was warm in her sweater but Hans swung his arms to keep warm. She said he could borrow something from one of the soldiers or even go back to the cottage for a blanket but he shook his head. It wasn't all that cold.

They didn't say very much, at first, because both were thinking of that dying man back there. She wondered aloud if Doctor Leino weren't callous. Hans thought it was simply the attitude of a pragmatic old professional.

'He wouldn't let the man die if he thought there was a chance to save him. But he doesn't appear to me to be very sorry that he *will* die.'

'I know his reasons. I've heard them recited over and over again.'

'Helene . . .'

'Yes?'

'I'm sorry it was so unpleasant for you.'

'It is over now, Hans.'

'Helene will you marry me?'

He said it too suddenly and it was also irrelevant to what they'd been saying; she stopped in her tracks and looked at him. He was defensive right away.

'I've wanted to ask it for a long while. If this isn't the proper time nor place, at least it got said.'

'Hans; what of your education and the other things — your home, parents . . . ?'

'We'll go to Essen. I'll finish the last year. I don't really want to, now, but it would be a shame after all these years to drop out with only one more year. Then we'll start out from there.'

He looked so sober she felt like smiling. From up front Doctor Leino, looking back, called to them.

'Come along; if you must argue wait until you're back in the village.'

Helene took his fingers in her cold grip and pulled. She hadn't answered him; she didn't, in fact, answer him. She simply said, 'Why, Hans? You didn't seem to want that last night or the night before. Why now — or have you talked to — someone?'

He was puzzled again. 'Talked to — whom? What would talking to anyone have to do with it? I've told you how much I love you, Helene. Isn't that enough? I've thought out a way for us to make it work.' He paused, being very honest on this score. 'Well; at least I'll *try* to make it work. Down in Essen we won't have much trouble finding a decent place to live, and if we work at it, we'll be happy, Helene.'

'It would be very hard on you, Hans, having a family, a wife, while you were in school.'

'No. Lots of people are married and still attending school.'

They emerged from the trees and started down the slight incline towards the village. There were a few lights here and there but for the most part Joki was dark. In the farther distance where starshine reflected off water, the river ran mindlessly towards its own quiet destiny. Someone had a wood-fire going; they could detect the diluted fragrance. It was probably one of the farmers living on the outskirts.

The soldiers relaxed a little once they were out of the forest. Doctor Leino had got another smoke from someone and was pacing along now swinging his battered old valise as though he were out for an evening stroll. He seemed to be an indefatigable person. The captain, on the other hand, although staying abreast of the physician, stumped along mechanically, but then he'd covered many more miles the day before, hadn't even had the forty winks Doctor Leino'd managed to get before being routed out by Helene, and furthermore, he had more on his mind than just one man.

A dog barked excitedly as the men trooped down among the little roads.

They halted in the centre of town, Doctor Leino buttoning his jacket under his chin and looking round for Helene who was coming farther back, still hand-in-hand with her tall, handsome young man. He watched them a moment as though arriving at a private conclusion, then said, 'Captain; if you call down to Raanujarvï tonight — excuse me — this morning, please ask that someone be sent up here to take Vendson back to the city. Dead or alive, he'll have to be got out of that cottage. And captain; one other thing: if the villagers are not told about their "Swede" perhaps he'll be permitted to go off in peace. I personally don't much care what they do to the man — yet a lot of things that are fresh in people's minds even now, after so many years have passed, are hardly worth having additional trouble over. What good can come of someone going up there and sticking a knife in him, or shooting him, to avenge a friend or brother? None at all. But the villager would be in serious trouble. So let us just say nothing and the man will die, and no one will be in trouble, eh?'

The officer nodded. 'What of the young man and the girl?'

'I'll talk to them. I'm sure they won't want to discuss Vendson anyway.'

'All right. Good night, Doctor.'

Leino nodded, turned and went back where Hans and Helene stood. They were both very grave, which seemed a little ridiculous to Doctor Leino to whom not many things were still solemn at his age, not likely to be permanent enough to make much difference anyway.

He explained his ideas about Vendson. They agreed without hesitation. He then said, perhaps a trifle embarrassed, 'I'm not pitying the man, but when you've seen as much death as I have, you'll perhaps wonder if everything people do wrong isn't such a very tiny ripple in the ocean of consciousness that it can't make any difference anyway, so let them go on without any last-minute recriminations.' He squinted as though not really expecting this statement to mean much — and it didn't — to the young people. 'Well; young lady — shall we go home now? It will be time for breakfast in another couple of hours, and if we're silent about getting into the house, we may still be able to get a little sleep without being grilled by your parents.'

Helene turned. Hans smiled softly, felt for her

hand, found it and squeezed. She squeezed back. Doctor Leino watched them keenly and cleared his throat. Helene turned and walked away. Doctor Leino kept staring at Hans a moment longer, then joined her. Their footfalls sounded loud in the hush and darkness.

CHAPTER FIFTEEN

Doctor Leino Betrays A Trust

By nine o'clock all the soldiers had returned to the village along with the injured and exhausted villagers. Three particularly hardy — or vindictive — men from Joki had refused to return; those three were on the trail of the shattered small remnant of escaping brigands.

Some concern was voiced but the captain was sanguine. 'Unless they are shot at by the troops infiltrating towards where the brigands last were, I should imagine that they will be safe enough. Certainly, since they are now alert enough not to be ambushed, and their numbers equal the number of remaining brigands, I wouldn't worry too much.'

The wounded had a sorry tale to tell of duplicity. It was difficult for the older people to accept the fact of Eric's treachery even when they had it in vehement statements from friends and kinsmen, and but for Doctor Leino's careful precautions to the contrary, several would have gone at once to the cabin in the forest except that, by order of the captain, his sergeant growled rough orders that no one from the village was to go up there under any circumstances.

The sergeant, using the imagination possessed by all old soldiers, said the sentry left there with

Vendson had been directed to fire his automatic weapon on sight. There'd been no such order given but the villagers didn't know it.

They gathered out front of Gunnar Mainpaa's store to listen to the tale of fighting by the survivors of the Joki contingent, and when Helene came down to open her father's establishment, she listened and wondered if already what had at best been a sorry little fight wasn't beginning to assume the proportions of an heroic legend.

She left the door open, went round to the desk, and Hans appeared as if by magic in the doorway. He was about to enter when Doctor Leino ambled up, touched the youth's shoulder and jerked his head. Hans turned away even before Helene had seen him. He and Pacius Leino walked along skirting the crowd out front of Mainpaa's establishment without a word passing between them. Doctor Leino looked infinitely more grave now, than he'd looked when he'd struggled under impossible conditions the night before to save a life.

No one heeded the two men. The village was once again in a mood of tense excitement. Doctor Leino said, 'Well; all the old heroes are vindicated, eh?' and smiled a little at his own comment.

Hans did not comment until they were down in the vicinity of the log hostel then he stopped. 'Whatever it is you have to say can be said here, or do we have to walk to the next town?'

Doctor Leino looked as though he'd have been

145

willing to walk on. He stopped and gazed back up where the crowd was, out front of Mainpaa's building. He looked up the rearward hill where a dying man lay — if he were not dead by this time — and only spoke when a light lorry came wending up towards them from the southerly open country.

'That will be the ambulance for our SS man, I suppose. They'll want me to certify his removal. Regulations.' He was being forced to say whatever had brought him this far and he didn't seem too pleased about that. '*Herr* Einhorst; last night you proposed marriage to Helene Vasaanen.'

Hans's eyes widened slightly as though in surprise, then narrowed quickly in resentment. Leino held up a hand.

'No,' he went on, 'I'm not meddling. At least not in the customary manner; I'm not just an inquisitive old man. Well; tell me this — did she agree to marry you or not?'

'She didn't answer. But what business is — ?'

'Wait; before you become angry listen to me. I can tell you something.'

'Then tell me,' said Hans, looking away only when the vehicle rolled past.

'She doesn't want to marry you. Maybe that's not entirely true; maybe I should have said she doesn't feel that she *should* marry you.'

Hans said, 'Go on, Doctor.'

'She is pregnant.'

Hans blinked but otherwise showed nothing until, a moment later, he slowly clenched his fists. But it was such a small thing perhaps it would have gone unobserved except that part of the doctor's trade was being observant. He lit a cigarette, blew smoke and looked straight into the eyes of the younger man.

'I wondered last night why she fainted so long after the mess. I took the liberty of testing a hunch about that. Last night when she and I left you and walked home, I stopped out front of her house and told her she was putting some innocent people in jeopardy by trying to conceal that which no woman has ever yet successfully concealed.'

'Doctor, are you very certain of this?'

Leino inhaled, exhaled, looked a little caustic and said, 'What kind of a physician do you think I am, *Herr* Einhorst?'

'Well . . .'

'Well indeed. Now let's pass over that childish question.'

'Why didn't she tell me?'

'That's exactly the point, *Herr* Einhorst; she thought she'd be forcing you into something. It seems — as near as I could discover — that you'd already told her of your future plans, and these plans did not include either a wife or a family. She is a proud girl; she wouldn't have told you after that. She wants no husband who pities her or worse yet, who marries her out of a sense of duty.'

Hans moved away, stepping into some morning shade near the log hostel. He put a hand upon the wall and leaned there with his back to Doctor Leino. The physician watched, then said, '*She* wouldn't tell you, and if her parents know, they wouldn't be likely to tell you either. So that left me to betray a girl's trust and become in her eyes as treacherous as that — that German up there in the forest. Well; now I've become something not very nice, but at least you *know*, which it seems to me you were entitled to do. Now, *Herr* Einhorst, it's all up to you. Goodbye.'

Doctor Leino turned and walked purposefully back up where the light ambulance was standing out front of Mainpaa's store with people crowding around it, with soldiers and their officers talking heatedly with the driver, who looked tired and irritable.

Once, Doctor Leino looked back. Hans was still down there in the shade beside the hostel but now he was gazing up towards the centre of town. Doctor Leino paused to drop his cigarette, step on it, then resumed his walk. Whatever he thought was not reflected upon his lined, tough face until the captain of soldiers saw him and stepped forth impatiently to demand where he'd been, saying a trifle angrily they'd all been waiting so he could go up with them while they brought Vendson down as far as the ambulance could go.

Doctor Leino shrugged in the face of the officer's annoyance. 'What's the hurry?' he asked. 'But if you are anxious to get back to Raanujarvï then let us go get your man. Although I'm confident we won't need soldiers for that chore. Not now.'

The ambulance driver evidently knew Doctor Leino quite well because he came over saying, 'I'd as soon get back to civilization before nightfall, Doctor, if you have no objections.'

Instead of replying Pacius Leino climbed into the ambulance and gestured. 'What are we waiting for?'

The captain and four soldiers got into the back of the vehicle leaving behind the sergeant and all the other soldiers. The last man in was the driver. He grimaced as the captain pointed the way up to the forest. He wanted to know how far they'd have to walk.

Doctor Leino sighed. 'Exercise is all that keeps people alive nowadays, yet you are afraid of a little walk.'

'Not the walk,' growled the driver, eyeing the forest. 'I don't like being boxed in. Forests do that to me.'

'Then discipline yourself,' said the physician as the vehicle jarred to a stop and everyone piled out and at once began walking through the gloom and shadows. 'The biggest fear men have, my friend, is fear itself.'

'Is that so?' exclaimed the driver acidly. 'Then why all the soldiers, Doctor?'

Leino looked at the younger man. 'You'll see. This corpse is heavy as lead.'

'Corpse?' echoed the captain.

Leino didn't reply.

They covered the distance soon enough; they went by a direct route this time with daylight to aid them. That soldier they'd left to guard the cabin the night before was standing in the doorway watching their approach long before they even got within hailing distance.

The captain stopped, eyed the soldier's glum countenance and stepped past into the cabin. The last man in was the ambulance driver. He craned over at the bed as Doctor Leino strolled over and without touching Vendson, bent to study his face. That only took a moment. He turned to the guard.

'Did he say anything before he died?'

The soldier nodded. 'He talked a little. But I don't understand German.'

The doctor was cheerful. 'Good. Then whatever his secrets were they will be buried with him, which is the way those things should be.' He gazed at the driver. 'Would you like to have to carry this body back down alone?'

It took the four soldiers to pick Vendson up and start back with him. Leino sent the driver after them. He and the captain went into the back room, bundled the effects from the metal-bound box and took them along. As the unburdened guard waited, the officer handed him the bundle. 'Take care of it,' he ordered. 'Not that it's going to prove any great revelation, but the authorities will want to know.'

He and Doctor Leino walked back for the last

time side by side, leaving the forlorn little cabin in its clearing where dappled sunshine lay like new gold. 'Bury him in the uniform,' said the doctor, and at the officer's quizzical look he gestured. 'What difference does it make now? At least let the man be loyal — brigand and traitor though he was to the people who trusted him. At least let him be true to himself. Bury him in the damned uniform. It too should go deep into the ground.'

The captain only said it wouldn't be up to him, but he would make the recommendation. He also asked if Doctor Leino was going to ride back to Raanujarvï in the army lorry. The doctor said he would; that if he remained any longer in Joki everyone with a bunion would be hunting him up for free treatment. Furthermore, since the injured villagers had all been treated and would recover, there'd be no purpose in him lingering.

They reached the waiting ambulance. The driver was silent on the drive back down into the village. So were the soldiers but they were panting from their exertion and probably wouldn't have felt much like talking anyway.

The crowd was waiting. It too was hushed. There weren't as many anger-twisted faces as might have been expected. Perhaps because all those people had known the dead man a good many years and could recall things he'd done which hadn't been bad at all.

They wanted to see Vendson. The captain forbade it. As Doctor Leino accepted his leather valise from Kasimir Mainpaa he looked at several bandaged men in the crowd and smiled, then shook his head in a manner which said very clearly that he thought they had all been fools.

The captain elected to return to Raanujarvï in the ambulance; gave orders for the sergeant to load the men into the lorry and follow after. He waved genially and perhaps a little condescendingly at the crowd and sat back as the ambulance worked through the press of villagers.

Near the lower end of town Doctor Leino leaned out as they were gathering momentum and called out to a handsome young man still standing in the shade of the empty hostel.

'Be true to your conscience, *Herr* Einhorst. Always be true to your conscience!'

It was by this time early afternoon with the heat at its zenith. Some of the crowd drifted away until the front of Mainpaa's store had perhaps no more than fifteen or twenty people still idling about. Next door a few people walked in and out of the Vasaanen store. Hans watched them. It took him that long to get his thoughts sorted out.

It was hard to understand a girl with so much pride, but he achieved the understanding and it left him feeling more humble than troubled. He also wondered at his good fortune; he had in his short manhood known quite a number of girls but never one like this. He began to speculate how many women a man had to know to find one like this, but because he was only in his twenties he couldn't know the answer, which in fact the vast majority of men, old and grey, didn't know either.

But he knew what he had to do. Not because honour demanded it but because *he wanted it!*

CHAPTER SIXTEEN

The Departure Of Hans

Franz Vasaanen recovered rapidly for someone his age. Marta disapproved of his walking only two days after the injury but, as he demonstrated, with the aid of crutches he made out very well. Furthermore, he fretted about the store. Helene assured him she was doing rather well without help but Franz had something else on his mind which he spoke of after supper when Marta was in the downstairs bedroom preparing the big old double-bed for him.

'I know his name now, Helene. Hans Einhorst. I saw him the day they brought me home. No, no, you needn't deny it. I saw the way he watched you. He is the one all right.'

Helene dreaded this confrontation with her father less now than before. She said, 'He asked me to marry him.'

'You will not,' said Franz.

She was surprised. 'You and mother don't want the shame; then of course I'll marry him.'

'*No!* We can devise some other way, but you will not marry this, this *German,* simply to protect your mother and me.'

She stared. 'But — has it occurred to you that I love him, father?'

'Hah! You are a good girl, Helene. A very, very

154

pretty and vital girl. Well; I am not so old that I don't know what it's like to be with someone desirable in the springtime. But neither your mother nor I will allow you to sacrifice yourself to salvage our honour. . . . You say you love him, but I know what you are doing and I won't allow it.'

Helene began to feel indignant. She was being treated as a child. Whatever she might have said was cut off by the appearance of Marta in the doorway saying she thought Franz should go to bed now, get some rest so that his recovery from the recent ordeal would be all that much quicker.

He pecked Helene on the cheek and departed, swinging his injured leg easily, without touching the floor with it at all.

Helene sat a while then arose to also retire but her mother came into the room saying Franz was upset. She didn't use it as an accusation at all, merely as a statement of fact. She also offered to fetch them both a cup of coffee but Helene declined and told her mother what she had also told her father.

Marta was less stubborn but evidently Franz had spoken to her for now she said, 'Marriage is a very long time, Helene. If you do something at the outset simply to prevent grief to others, long after the grief will be forgot, the obligation will still exist. I think your father is right. I think we'll just have to find some other —'

'Mother, I love him.'

Marta sat in the chair her husband had vacated. She studied her daughter a moment. 'Are you very sure, Helene?'

'Mother; if I hadn't been very sure . . . that other time . . . I wouldn't be in this condition now. I love him more than I can describe. That's what I tried to explain to Father but he wouldn't believe me.'

'It would be natural for your father to resent this young man intensely. You are his only child — his only daughter. I remember hearing it said many years ago that no father believes any man, no matter how good or exalted, is good enough for his daughter.'

'Mother; he asked me to marry him and I'm going to accept.'

'Does he know . . . ?'

'I haven't told him but I will tomorrow.'

Marta sighed with strong fatalism. 'I hope with all my heart it doesn't make a difference, Helene.'

'Why should it?'

Marta shrugged. 'Men are men,' she muttered, and arose as though there was nothing more to be discussed. 'When will you see him?'

'Tomorrow.'

Marta nodded, still looking glum, bade her daughter good night and went off to bed. Helene, less perturbed than puzzled by the sudden change in her mother's attitude, went up the stairs very slowly. If her mother had said something negative she could have combated it, but there was no way to speak out against something unless one knew precisely what it was that had to be combated.

She slept well despite her anxiety. She also awakened refreshed and alert. In fact she felt much better, now that she'd come to her decision, than she'd felt in several days. She even thought charitably of Doctor Leino whose keen observation had detected her dilemma. But most of all, she was glad Doctor Leino was gone; not that she didn't trust his discretion, but because she didn't want to have to endure another stern lecture such as the one he'd given her outside the house the night they'd walked home together. He was both blunt — and right — a combination scarcely likely to endear him to anyone he was remonstrating with.

He'd insisted she tell Hans. All her arguments to the contrary had been what he'd called 'specious'. He'd said the longer she waited the worse it was going to be next spring when the child was born. He'd also scolded her for being naïve enough to think that she could carry the whole burden herself.

'You consider yourself heroic right now, young lady, and capable of carrying on all by yourself, but let me tell you that no business establishment in one of the large cities will keep you working in an office when you begin to swell. Then where will you be — unable to support yourself, unable to return to your village?'

She completed bathing, dressing, putting up

her hair and thought of Hans in the starlight when he'd asked her to marry him. She smiled. He'd been so uncomfortable yet so very serious and solemn. It was possible for her to feel protective towards him; he'd been so unsure yet so brave. She'd always considered him strong but in this instance she'd seen his courage at its limit and that made her want to help him.

When she was lying in bed she knew a tenderness that went with genuine affection. It was the first time since she'd known him that she hadn't felt torn by conflict, bruised by shame, harassed by guilt. Now, having arrived at her decision she could see everything differently.

The following morning she went down to open the store a trifle earlier than usual. There was a crispness to the day even after the sun began its climb and golden light lay all around. It was too early for autumn but in the north country winter very often announced its nearness well in advance of its actual arrival.

She liked the cold, always had. It made her cheeks rosy, her beautiful eyes sparkle, her step lighter and longer.

She built a small fire to take the chill out of the store then went to the desk to work at the books. Her father had taught her how to make out the statements, how to operate the purchase, profit and loss columns. She rather liked this part of storekeeping. During the fierce winters she'd work at her desk in crackling warmth and in the hot mid-summers she'd be where it was cool.

But today her mind kept wandering. She finally closed the books and waited. But Hans did not appear. Other people did, including several of the 'veterans' of the fight with the brigands. They had grand stories to relate and small purchases to make, usually of liniment of gauze or salve. One man had been injured in a very embarrassing manner and this, after all the anxiety had died down, became a point of high glee. He'd been stooping over to retrieve a weapon he'd dropped when a bullet had caught him through one ham. Without using words that might offend, Helene was informed of this matter no less than four times before noon, but by then she was no longer interested in any of the tales. Hans hadn't come round.

Kasimir Mainpaa came for some tinned things and she asked if he'd seen Hans that morning. He hadn't. Later, about one-thirty, Eino came for tobacco and she asked him; he hadn't seen the tall youth either. At three o'clock Kasimir returned to ask a question:

'Why would Jannes Wilko buy tobacco if he doesn't smoke?'

Helene answered simply, 'His wife smokes.'

Kasimir's face cleared as though by magic; evidently, for some reason she didn't try to fathom, this riddle had been bothering the crippled nephew of the mayor of Joki. Then Kasimir said, 'After you asked about the German I looked, but his bicycle was not down at the hostel and neither was he. In fact, where he had his little camp, it was all bare and empty.'

Her heart stopped beating for a second.

'They come and go, Helene,' said Kasimir, watching her face, slightly curious, also slightly pitying. 'Well; I am sorry.' He hitched along to the door and disappeared beyond.

She stood like stone for a long while looking out where golden sunlight lay. People passing left wisps of conversation near the doorway which she didn't hear. Village life seemed almost back to normal. This was the first day in some time since there'd been no soldiers, no armed villagers, passing back and forth. Of course the conversation respecting Eric Vendson wouldn't atrophy for a long while yet to come, but it would most certainly become secondary to other more current and pertinent topics.

She was drawn to the door and stood there looking southward towards the lower end of town. The log hostel was shaded by that huge old trimmed tree down there, but it had the appearance of an uninhabited place.

He knew.

She could guess who had told him; she could also imagine how that informant had scolded him precisely as he'd scolded her. She felt less resentment towards Doctor Leino than depressing disillusionment in Hans.

At least the doctor had felt he'd been doing the right thing. If his intentions, good though they'd been, had instead sent Hans away from the suffocating entanglement of her pregnancy and what it would mean later on to a college student, she couldn't actually blame the doctor even when she'd have given ten years off her life if *she,* not Doctor Leino, had told Hans.

She returned to the desk beyond the counter, sank down there, placed both elbows hard down and rested her chin in cupped palms. From her earlier mood of pleasant, warm empathy, she sank into a grey despair. But being in love made it possible for her to understand Hans's departure.

She perhaps should have felt abandoned, deserted, entirely alone, and in time of course that mood would appear, but sitting in the early twilight at closing time without a soul besides herself in the store, she only felt like weeping for something very beautiful, tender and gentle, which had apparently gone out of her life forever.

Trygve Vesainen came in with a jacket buttoned to his throat. He smiled, asked for cigarettes, then dropped a casual statement. 'I saw the young man with the bicycle pedalling away for all he was worth down towards Raanujarvï. I was coming back to the village in my car and he was of course going in the opposite direction or I'd have given him a lift.'

She smiled mechanically, handed over the smokes, took Trygve's money and turned away as though unwilling to talk. Vesainen lingered though, opening the packet, extracting a cigarette and lighting it. He looked relaxed and totally at ease, which of course he was since he hadn't seen her expression nor guessed her mood.

'Well; it is now all over, Helene. We did what we should have done ten years ago. They told me down at Raanujarvï the soldiers caught the three or four brigands still in the forest and that the men from Joki who were pursuing them should arrive back in town late tonight or in the morning.' He looked at her through the lazy smoke. 'Tell your father, will you?'

She nodded and Trygve departed.

It was after five o'clock, shadows were settling in, her world was a shambles at her feet, she dreaded going home but went through all the mechanical functions necessary to secure the store for the night, and afterwards, with a sweater round her shoulders, began the short walk.

Up until now she'd felt too numb for tears but the chill evening air, or the exertion, or perhaps just the adequate passage of time which permitted the shock to turn to deep-down anguish, finally allowed the tears to flow. She walked steadily along without making a sound with tears running down each cheek and splashing on the ground underfoot.

She only made a real effort to stop weeping when she saw the lights ahead in her house, but it took a little time to regain control. Even then, she knew her mother would see the redness at once, so when she entered through the front door she did so very surreptitiously, then ran upstairs to bathe her face before suppertime.

CHAPTER SEVENTEEN

The Edge Of Tragedy

The hammerblow fell the following morning. She knew it the moment she saw her father and Trygve Vesainen talking in the doorway, Trygve acting casual as he conversed, her father slowly coming to a stiff, attentive posture despite the crutches. She could almost guess the exact words '. . . pedalling down towards Raanujarvï as fast as he could go. . . .'

She forced her attention back to the books, then arose with a glassy smile when two women entered seeking soap and lye and other similar impedimenta to good housecleaning. She was still waiting on them when her father entered, white to the eyes and scarcely able to respond to the greetings casually offered by the women shoppers. Formerly, Helene had wished only for the two women to complete their shopping and go away. Now, she prolonged their stay with conversation, with suggestions and offerings from the laden shelves.

But eventually they would depart; she knew it and braced for what came as soon as they'd gone. Her father was at the desk, crutches put aside, shoulders drooping, weathered, tight-drawn face towards the yonder morning sun-shine. She began to think he wasn't going to speak but she was wrong.

In a very quiet tone he said, 'He is gone, Helene, and it doesn't surprise me. After all, young men are like young stags. They roam at will; tying one down isn't as easy as you probably thought it would be.' He raised anguished eyes. 'You are a good girl; you wanted to do the right thing.' He clenched a fist atop the desk. 'We will make arrangements.'

She wanted to ask what 'arrangements' but considering the grimness of his visage decided to say nothing at all. Fortunately, Jannes Wilko shuffled in for tobacco. Remembering Kasimir Mainpaa's interest in this matter she went after the packet for Jannes and asked about his wife; had she completely recovered from her ordeal the night the brigands came. Jannes said she had; that in fact she was now more relaxed than she'd been in a long while; that this was due entirely to the fact that the outlaws had been swept away to a man.

He also said an army vehicle had returned the last villager to Joki after the final pursuit and dispersal of the brigands. He called a pleasant greeting to her father who didn't seem to hear, paid for the tobacco and departed, throwing a slightly puzzled, mildly affronted look at Franz who hadn't acknowledged Jannes's presence at all.

Helene began feeling better. It usually happened that way with her when adversity reached its climax. At first she suffered, then she became philosophical, and finally she took the initiative as she now did.

'I've said before, Father, I won't bring shame to you. I won't. Whatever you have planned, don't worry about it. I've already made up my mind to go down to the city and get a job. I'm a good book-keeper.'

He looked at her in much the same manner as had Doctor Leino. 'What kind of book-keeper — with a big belly, Helene? No; that wouldn't be any answer. I'm not concerned with the shame as much as with *you*.' He looked round for his crutches, gripped them as though to arise, then sat a moment longer to say, 'We'll all go down to one of the big cities in a few days. Perhaps next week when my leg is better and I can walk without these things. We'll find you a nice apartment. Your mother can stay with you for a while. And later on . . . when the time is near . . . she will stay with you until it's all over.' He stood, propped himself on the crutches and shook his head in the face of whatever she was about to say. 'Never mind. We have the money. What good is money if it's not used to care for one's own family? Now don't argue. Today I'm not up to it.' He looked away from her, out into the roadway and started swinging himself doorward. 'You can close the store early if you wish. There isn't going to be much business anyway.'

After he'd gone she leaned on the counter looking at the doorway through which he'd passed feeling dirty and dishonest as though she'd done a terrible thing to the parents who'd loved and trusted her. The tears stung but she held them back.

She did close the store early but instead of going home she wandered aimlessly down to the hostel with its sad memories. She even walked out through that small wood behind the building which twisted and turned until it fetched up where fishing boats were turned wrong side up when not in use. There, she even sat upon the same hummock of salt-grass where she'd sat the last time they'd been there together.

There was another place but it seemed sordid now to even think of it let alone to go there.

Water lapped at the nearby shore, birds wheeled and mournfully called, trees upon a little island not far out bent before a southerly wind that didn't reach the shore at all. The sun was warm and caressing. Under any other circumstances it would have been a lovely day, a lovely spot. Now, it was full of a paralysing kind of bitterness for while she didn't *want* to believe Hans had abandoned her there was little else for her to think.

What excuse could he have offered had he suddenly materialized beside her? She could think of none; even if he'd had one, how could he explain his reason for not telling her?

Kasimir Mainpaa came up along the shore carrying a book. She saw him first and tried to make up her mind to flee. He hadn't seen her but of course he would detect movement. She sat hoping against hope that he'd miss her, but of course no such good fortune would have befallen her on this day of days.

He saw her, stopped as though surprised, squinted, then altered his crabbed course to approach. As a child she'd feared Kasimir because of his deformity. Later, as a healthy growing child she'd felt pity mixed with mild loathing, but now as a woman she felt nothing for Kasimir one way or another. She knew of course that the handicap prevented him from participating in any of the muscular, masculine endeavours of the village; she also knew — at least by hearsay — that Kasimir was scholarly. But beyond that, and the fact that his parents were dead, that Gunnar was his dead father's brother, she knew actually very little about him.

At this particular moment she didn't want to talk to him but there was now no way to avoid it. He came scuffing straight on up, stopped to study her in the waning light, and offered a little smile of greeting.

'I thought I was the only one who came down here, Helene. It is a private place when the fishermen aren't working with the boats.'

She nodded, struggling to match his capacity for small talk. 'Were you reading, Kasimir?'

He looked at the book as though he'd forgot he was carrying it. 'Very honestly,' he confided, 'I got so sick of hearing heroes I walked away from town. Yes, I was reading. Faulkner, the American.'

'Is he good?'

Kasimir looked again at the book. 'I suppose so, but it seems to me authors spend too much time trying to educate people to all the sordidness in life, when as a matter of fact anyone past thirty already has seen enough of it.'

She paused, letting the conversation hang up in the hope he might go on. But he didn't; he sank down near her and pointed to the little forested island out in the sooty evening. 'There is one of those old stone rings out there. Did you know that? My uncle says they were Viking watch-towers.' Kasimir dropped his hand and grinned a little. 'I don't argue with my uncle. But it seems to me the stone and mortar is more recent.' He looked up, studied her profile a moment then said, speaking very softly, 'Helene; I would kill him for you if I could.'

She was shocked and looked downward with a swift toss of her head. 'Kasimir; what are you talking about?'

'The handsome German. Helene; I know what it's like to love someone. I also know what it's like not to have someone return that love.'

'Kasimir!'

'No; don't be angry. We are just two people speaking of things that will go no further. I saw how you looked at him, how you smiled in a special way for him. I wouldn't have believed there could be a man who could do such a thing to you.'

'What — thing?' she asked in a low voice.

'Well; Trygve saw him riding away, down by Raanujarvï.'

'But — he wasn't riding *away*, particularly, Kasimir.'

The hunchback lowered his wise eyes to the book in his lap and muttered. 'No. Well; I don't blame you for not wanting to speak of it. The pain is deep. Believe me, Helene, I know.'

He got up with an effort, dusted his trousers and gripped his book. He offered to walk her back to the centre of the village because shadows were filling over the world now, very swiftly. She declined so he said, 'Don't sit here too long. The cold comes in about this time off the estuary. And your parents — if you haven't been home from the store yet — they'll worry.'

She suddenly felt great pity. He was a kindly person; observant and protective and kindly. 'I'll leave soon,' she said. 'Good night, Kasimir.'

He was right about more than just one thing too, for only a few minutes after he'd gone shambling up the crooked little path it did turn cold very suddenly as the wind changed and began coming straight inland.

She walked back without thinking of the fearsome shadows or the deep hush. At the hostel she turned up towards the edge of town then kept right on going as far as the house with the lighted windows and the smell of cooking coming out as far as the roadway.

Her father was reading and looked up rather sharply when she entered. She saw in his face he was trying to decide whether or not to demand to know where she'd been so late. She smiled at him, walked out into the kitchen and Marta said, 'We didn't hold up supper for you. Sit down, I've kept things warm. Where have you been?'

'For a walk down by the river.'

Marta said no more on that subject. She became very busy with dishes and pans. She set food in front of Helene, drew herself a cup of coffee and sat opposite her daughter at the spotless old kitchen table, her face lined with worry, and tired looking.

'Your father told me the boy has left,' Marta said. 'If that's so, then you mustn't worry too much.'

It dawned on Helene what her mother was thinking; that she might do something desperate. She stopped eating for a moment. She had, by delaying her return home, frightened her parents whose thoughts were on things girls in her position sometimes did. She lost all appetite; she'd once again brought pain and anxiety to her parents.

She wanted to say something but didn't know the words so she reached over and patted her mother's hand. 'I wouldn't do anything foolish, Mother. You know me better than that.'

Marta relaxed. She even made a feeble little smile. 'That's what I said to your father. Well; men are all worriers.' Marta stopped speaking for a moment. 'Some men at any rate — the decent ones.'

Helene arose to refill her mother's cup and take dishes to the sink. 'Were you surprised to learn about Eric, Mother?'

Marta nodded. 'Everyone was. I'll tell you what I think; that Eric was two men. One, a decent, lonely man, the other something a bad environment made him into. I've heard all the cursing but personally, I feel very sorry for him. I tell you, Helene, living is not as easy as people make believe that it is. Staying *alive* isn't as hard as *living*. For one you need sharp wits and resourcefulness, but what you need for the other only God knows, I certainly don't.'

Helene finished clearing the table, washed and dried and shelved the dishes then sat down again. She felt tired for no particular reason. Tired and drained dry. She said she thought she'd go to bed. Marta understood, kissed her and went to the parlour door to watch Helene kiss her father, be kissed in return, then go heavily up the stairs to her room. Marta lustily blew her nose and went into the parlour where she and Franz exchanged a look. He nodded, closed his book and reached for his crutches.

'If I'm to get an early start in the morning with Trygve, I'll need to get to bed.'

She didn't help him although she stood as though she might offer to. Franz didn't need any help. He cursed the crutches, which was a good sign, and went into the bedroom with Marta behind him. There, he took the oily Luger pistol from a box and looked at it.

Marta said, 'It isn't right, Franz. I've said that fifty times this afternoon. What good will it do?'

'It will keep that young man from ever doing such a thing again to decent people, Marta, that's what it will accomplish.'

He put the gun on a chair, sat down and began undressing. His wife went round on the far side to do the same. She said, 'Do you know what Helene will think? That she drove you to this. That will make her feel worse than she feels now. Franz; we should *protect* her, not try to avenge her.'

He didn't answer.

CHAPTER EIGHTEEN

A Time Of Worry

He was gone the following morning when Helene arose and went downstairs to make a light breakfast, then head for the store. She thought both her parents had over-slept because not even her mother was up and about, which was unusual but not altogether unheard of. Anyway, it didn't matter to Helene; they'd probably talked late.

She felt better, but then, first thing in the morning, she usually felt good. The day was fresh, the sunlight new, the world cleansed by dew and night-winds. It was nearly impossible despite one's problems, not to feel kinship with a new day.

There was more business this morning than there'd been in days. She thought perhaps it was occasioned by the fact that the excitement had quite abated by this time and people were finding they'd eaten up their reserves in the cupboards.

It was also pleasant being busy, but that came as no revelation; she'd long ago discovered the therapeutic value of keeping busy. In the intervals between shoppers she worked a little on the books although they were up-to-date now, fully current and balanced.

She had little reason to think of herself, of

Hans, of anything personal at all in fact, until Gunnar came in, a small white patch on the side of his head where the wound was healing and asked for her father. She said he was at home and old Gunnar left.

Fifteen minutes later she was standing in the doorway when Mainpaa came walking past. 'Find him?' she asked pleasantly. He looked a little sour as he replied.

'No, but then if he'd told you he was going down to Raanujarvï I would have been saved the walk.'

She pronounced the name of the town with her lips and didn't make a sound. Gunnar went on past, ducked into his adjoining store and was lost to sight. Two women with shawls, carrying knit shopping bags, came to the doorway and waited for Helene to allow them to enter. She was busy with them for almost twenty minutes. Both were good customers and heavy purchasers. After they'd departed she went back to the door to stand in the sunlight.

There was a perfectly logical reason for her father to go down to Raanujarvï — his wounded leg. But she knew that hadn't been the reason; the leg was coming along splendidly and her father wouldn't have made the trip just for that reason anyway; he was no lover of doctors in any case.

Of course he might have gone down there to make purchases for the store, but that didn't hold water even as it occurred to her; in the first place he'd bought for the store only a short while back. In the second place he'd have said something to her since she'd been keeping track of the inventory. In the final analysis, he wouldn't have known what they were low on because he hadn't been in the store except to visit since he'd been wounded.

That left just one possible reason for his going to Raanujarvï or so it seemed to her. Without bothering to close the store she went to the Vesainen residence and asked for Trygve. Mrs. Vesainen said, looking mildly surprised at the question, that her husband had driven Franz Vasaanen to the city; that they'd left before sunup. When Helene was trying to think up some way to determine whether Mrs. Vesainen knew *why* they'd gone down there, the older woman said, 'They will be back shortly. Trygve would have told me if it'd been anything important.'

Trygve Vesainen, then, hadn't known why Helene's father had wanted to visit Raanujarvï. She turned and walked back to the store to think. She was sure *she* knew why her father had gone.

At noon she locked the front door and went home. Marta was knitting, red-eyed and distraught. Helene said nothing as she and her mother looked at one another. She walked on through into the downstairs bedroom, went to the box where the Luger was kept and opened it. There was no gun in the box. She turned. Marta was standing in the doorway.

Helene said quietly, 'Why, Mother; for his honour or mine?'

Marta didn't reply; she turned and went heavily back to the parlour, sat down and picked up her knitting again. She'd lost the ability to cope with the problem and had turned to her own private release, knitting.

Helene went to the telephone, called Doctor Leino's office down in Raanujarvï, got the physician on the third ring and crisply told him what she suspected. Doctor Leino listened politely then said, 'All right; but if the boy rode down here yesterday morning it is very unlikely he's still here. In any case I'll go see if I can find your father. As for anyone being shot — I wouldn't worry very much if I were you. This is a large city, young lady, one old man with a bad leg isn't going to be able to cover all of it even with the use of his friend's automobile.'

'Doctor — the police?'

Leino was dubious. 'I don't think that'll be necessary. It certainly won't look very good if they were brought into it. If necessary, perhaps, later on, but first let me see what I can do.'

'Doctor be careful, please be very careful.'

The physician grunted, which could have meant anything or nothing, rang off and Helene went back into the parlour where her mother looked up; she'd heard one side of the conversation. Helene said, 'He'll find father. Also, he says it's improbable that father will find Hans — that if he reached the city yesterday morning he

176

probably is a long way from Raanujarvï by now.'

Marta put down the knitting. 'I told him it was foolish but he'd already made up his mind last night before bed time.'

Helene went to make them both some black coffee. She began to feel weak in the legs, not exclusively because of what might happen to her father or Hans, but because she was the cause.

The coffee tasted good but having Helene with her made the change in Marta. She put her knitting away and relaxed a little, looking dully resigned, acting less panicky now than just philosophical. 'What can he do in a big city with that wounded leg?' she asked garrulously. 'If the police catch him carrying that gun they'll arrest him.' She looked up. 'The best of men get very foolish sometimes, Helene.'

Someone knocked on the front door. Helene went to see what it was and what they wanted. It was the wife of Jannes Wilko who complained that she'd walked all the way into the village to make purchases at the store, and now it was closed. Helene called back to her mother where she was going and left the house with Mrs. Wilko who kept up a running fire of disjointed conversation all the way down to the centre of the village where Helene unlocked the store and let her customer inside.

After Mrs. Wilko had made her purchases and had gone, Marta appeared with a dark shawl over her shoulders although actually it was quite warm out. Helene put her mother to work filling shelves. For herself there was always something to do and when customers appeared she struck up light conversation; it didn't help very much but there was little else one could do and it at least helped the hours to pass.

At three o'clock Doctor Leino called. He sounded a little wry as he said he'd found Franz Vasaanen. 'I took away the silly gun and now I've got him on a couch because all that walking gave him a muscular spasm in the bad leg. Don't worry, young lady, he'll be home for supper. But I think I'll keep the Luger, at least for a while; when next I come to Joki I'll bring it back.'

Helene lowered her voice. 'And Hans, Doctor?'

'Well of course he wasn't to be found; I told you, in a town as large as this one even if he'd still been here, which is very improbable, he'd be difficult to locate. Don't worry. That is, don't worry about your foolish father.' Doctor Leino paused, then said something that wasn't entirely relevant but which appeared to have been in his private thoughts. 'These old idiots; because they ran off a small band of hungry brigands, now they think they'll set all Finland's — and their own — wrongs to right. What I should have done was hand him over to the police.'

'Doctor; what of the man who drove my father down there?'

'All right; he's eating in my kitchen. I haven't told him anything and evidently your father kept his secret too. This man thinks he came down

178

here to help your father locate an old friend. I'll see them on their way back shortly. And young lady — forget that young man.'

Helene replaced the receiver on its hook and turned to see Marta watching her. She related all that she'd been told and Marta looked greatly relieved. At once she denounced Helene's father.

'Making a fool of himself, that's what he's doing. Acting the fool. Everyone will laugh.'

'Mother, Doctor Leino isn't going to say anything and neither are you or I. That leaves only father. I'm sure he'll keep quiet. Then who will know he made a fool of himself?'

'I will,' muttered Marta. 'Going down to a place as big as Raanujarvï with a gun in his belt; who does he think he is — another Mannerheim?' Marta threw up her hands and lifted her eyes.

Helene smiled very softly. She understood how the fear could turn to recrimination in moments. She suggested they go home and prepare a supper that her father would like because he surely would be starved by the time he and Trygve returned to the village.

Marta was agreeable but then, like the knitting, at home and busying herself in the kitchen, was also as much nervous release as constructive endeavour for her. She told Helene several of Franz's favourite dishes as though Helene were a neighbour instead of an observer who'd sat at the same table all her life. She even showed Helene how to give the little personal touch to the things they prepared.

It was as a matter of fact a very pleasant time. No one mentioned Helene's condition, her trouble, the anxieties or worries of her parents, and most certainly no one mentioned Hans Einhorst.

It was as though they'd somehow managed to roll back time a month and everything was as it used to be. Marta even laughed a little and Helene related amusing anecdotes from the store. It was a good time for them both.

There could be no denying the fact that a woman's kitchen was in many ways also her confessional nave, her personal place of private therapy, her fortress against adversity and her creative studio. For Marta, who was older, the big old cheery room was also a morale builder.

She told Helene tales of her courtship and some things about Franz that his daughter had never heard before. Brave and ludicrous things. She also offered some trenchant observations such as the description of Franz which said that 'He was strong as a young man, and agreeable. He was also courageous, but he didn't like the killing nor the devastation. He once told me he didn't think the world could recover from the war in less than a hundred years. Well; of course the world recovered in less than twenty years, but your father saw cathedrals collapsed that had stood several centuries so he thought it would take that long again. You see, Helene? He was a good man, strong and loyal, but he was just an ordinary man with the limited perception of ordinary men.'

Helene smiled at her mother. The fact was, neither of her parents were exactly ordinary; she thought how un-ordinary it was for people to still love one another after thirty years of marriage.

Shadows fell, night came stalking down across the village from the yonder forest, stars brightened, the moon, thicker, more opalescent now, shed a vaster light and up and down the main road of the village lights burned in the houses.

Across the road a dog barked furiously and Marta went to lift aside a curtain and peer out. They'd heard no auto but then Trygve might let Franz walk the little distance from the shed where he housed his vehicle. But Marta saw nothing and returned to her work.

They set the table carefully, killing time, and gradually they said less and less to each other. The cheery period was past, reality crowded in again along with the ghostly moonlight, forest-shadows, and the long, long hush.

When the dog stopped barking they forgot him. Then he started up again and this time someone knocked on the front door. Helene was nearest the kitchen's exit so she walked on through the parlour. Marta remained in the kitchen.

Helene swung back the panel and stood perfectly still. Hans said, smiling down into her face, 'Can I come in?'

She put one hand to her throat. The other hand remained upon the door. She got a little dizzy and her heart pounded. Marta called from the kitchen, 'Is it your father?'

Helene closed the door, turned her back and leaned upon it. 'No, Mother.'

CHAPTER NINETEEN

The Return Of Hans

It was almost ten o'clock when Franz limped in looking depressed and pained. Marta at once sat him at the supper table and scolded him. He drank a cup of coffee and within moments seemed more lively. Marta had laced it with brandy.

Helene was unusually quiet through the long meal. She ate because of hunger and that at least gave her some excuse for being so silent. It did not, however, give her an excuse for being so pale.

Marta told her husband he had wasted an entire day, had taken up the time of a number of otherwise busy people, and had accomplished nothing. He listened without saying a word, but when he was half through the meal and had drunk his second cup of laced coffee, his eyes brightened and his colour returned.

'Of course you are right, but people do things impulsively, you know.'

'With guns in their pockets, Franz?'

He didn't reply to that. So far, he'd avoided speaking to his daughter but now he did. 'I think perhaps we should go south within the next few days, Helene. Raanujarvï is too close; most of the villagers go there sometimes during the year. I was thinking of Helsinki. It is at the other end of the country, we will not see anyone down there we know.'

He talked almost casually, as though the reason for going that far away weren't the really important issue, which, perhaps, it no longer was for him now that he'd fully accepted it and had begun to think past it.

'Well,' he said, 'Helene; what do you think?'

The beautiful eyes lifted. 'Do we have to discuss it tonight?'

Marta intervened, still mildly bristling. 'Of course not. Tomorrow will be soon enough. Franz; you must go to bed and let me put fresh bandages on the wound.'

Franz shrugged. He *was* tired; replete and warm from the brandy and dog-tired. He left the table. Marta patted her daughter's hand, then arose and trailed along after him. Helene could hear their voices, low and quiet, in the far bedroom as she cleared the table with mechanical motions. From the kitchen she could hear nothing, nor did she try to.

As she washed dishes and dried them she tried to force order into her thinking. If her father had approached the house while Hans had been standing at the door. . . . What had brought him back: conscience, pity, shame? She hardened towards him on each score. She'd been very willing night before last, to marry him. Now, she felt as doggedly against the idea as she'd felt when first she'd known she was pregnant.

But something else troubled her; he wouldn't

leave in all probability until he'd seen her. That of course posited the one situation she wanted most to avoid now — a meeting between Hans and her father in broad daylight, which surely would happen.

She finished the dishes, ran upstairs for a sweater, then returned to the parlour, heard the low voices still coming from beyond the bedroom door where her parents were, and carefully let herself out of the house without a sound.

The night was bright enough to see part way down towards the centre of town. It was warm, too, but she wasn't aware of that as she tossed the sweater round her shoulders out of habit and started walking the full length of the village down towards the hostel where she was certain he would be.

It struck her that, from feeling desperate because he had gone to feeling desperate now he had returned, didn't really make very good sense. She attributed it to the inconsistencies of love and didn't try to reason beyond that.

Neither did she try to explain away her headlong rush to see him. That was love, pure and simple and she'd never denied that she was in love with him — totally and irrevocably. The only thing she *would* deny was that they had a future together. On the other hand, if things had happened differently — or, to put it better, if things *hadn't happened at all* — they would have had what she was convinced would have been a wonderful future together.

She passed her father's store, Mainpaa's building, several other business establishments; the moonlight seemed stronger down here, probably because there were no trees to reach skyward and obstruct light. She heard her own footfalls and glanced round as she walked, to find she was quite alone in the roadway. It was a fact that people who spent long winter evenings inside warm houses did not break the habit even in summertime. She smiled a little at that; she knew everyone in Joki and most of the people beyond who lived on farms or in isolated cabins. They were consistent in habit, in behaviour, in the pattern of their full and comfortable lives. Actually, she knew no other way of life although during her restless years she'd often wished she could experience the ways other people lived.

He was in the hostel doorway watching but her thoughts were objective enough to preclude her seeing him right away.

He said, 'Helene,' in a soft call.

She turned, saw him and slowed her gait slightly as he stood waiting. When she was closer he stepped out of the log building.

She could see his face; it was older-looking than it had been before, not of course in its texture but rather in its expression and in the way the blue eyes steadily regarded her. She thought she knew what he was thinking so, before he could speak, she said, 'Hans; why didn't you just keep going?'

'Going?' he asked. 'Going where?'

'Well; back to Essen — wherever you were —'

'Wait a moment, Helene. Who told you I was going back to Essen?'

'No one.'

'Then why did you think that?'

'Well,' she said defensively, seeing the steady but mild hostility in his gaze, 'isn't that where you were going?'

'Damn it, no, and I resent having it thrown up at me as though I were a coward fleeing from something.'

She stopped speaking and watched anger etch his lips and eyes with small lines. He seemed to have more to say but didn't say it. Instead, he fished a crumpled paper from a pocket and thrust it at her.

'Read it!'

She took the paper, stepped back away from the shadows out front of the hostel and bent to read. The paper was a crisp telegram; it said something to the effect that he must be very certain, very thoughtful and analytical, because marriage was the most serious decision he would make in his lifetime. It then said, 'But if you are sure, son, then marry her and hasten home to us.' It was signed: 'Mother and Father'.

She looked over at him. He said nothing even when she handed back the telegram and he shoved it into a pocket.

'Hans,' she whispered. 'Is that why you went away?'

He nodded. 'I rode down to Raanujarvï to

send a telegram to my parents. There is no office for such transmissions in Joki. I left very early yesterday morning because it's a long ride. I sent the message then rented a room in a small hotel and slept most of the day. When the answer came back, I then lay over until this morning and started back.'

She didn't trust her voice so she simply smiled at him, but he was still indignant. 'What was wrong about that? I'd asked you to be my wife the night before, when we returned from the forest. I wanted my parents to know. Is that a crime? You acted as though I'd done something terrible when I came to your house, tonight.'

'Hans I'm terribly sorry. I know how frightfully I acted but —'

'But,' he interrupted sharply. 'But what? Listen to me, Helene, I was completely bewildered by the way you acted. Until I learned *why*, then it made sense. Perhaps not too much sense, but then I'm not a girl so I wouldn't act the same way. At least I doubt if I would. But now that we have no secret between us — you slammed the door in my face tonight.' He shook his head at her. 'How many excuses must I make for you?'

'No more,' she murmured and went up to him, raised both hands and pulled his face down to her. 'Never again, Hans.'

The kiss was long and disturbing so when she released him she stepped back one step. 'Please understand. You said you had a year of school yet. You also said you'd return next summer.

But you see, Hans, I couldn't wait that long.'

'Yes of course I see — now — but I had no idea then. Not until Doctor Leino explained to me what had caused you to faint up there at the SS man's cabin.' He reached, took her hand and held it. 'And it wasn't duty or obligation or anything like that, Helene, because if you'll recall I asked you to marry me *before* Doctor Leino told me your condition.'

She nodded through a stinging mist and smiled. 'I thought I'd die when you went away. Why didn't you just say where you were going?'

He had no very good answer to that. 'I didn't think I'd be gone two full days, and neither did I think two days were going to cause all this trouble. I guess I just wasn't thinking things out too well, Helene, but then I had never asked a girl to marry me before, either.' He forced a little rueful smile and drew her in closer. She did not resist even when he crooked an arm around her shoulders and pushed back her head with his lips on her mouth.

Afterwards, she wanted to sit down. They went round to the south side of the hostel where his sleeping bag lay, still rolled, and she sat there while he utilized a round, smooth segment of sawn wood which had been cut and left there as a sort of stool.

He said, 'Now that the mysteries are cleared up — you still haven't answered my question, Helene.'

She was thankful for the darkness as she used a tiny handkerchief. 'I'll marry you, Hans. You knew the answer when you asked the question.'

He smiled and wagged his head. 'No I didn't. And when I asked it I'm not sure you knew the answer either.'

She didn't dispute that; she said, 'I'd better go back now,' and arose.

He watched her a moment before arising to say, 'Helene; I, uh, don't know too much about — these things — but mathematically it seems to me the sooner we are married the better. No?'

She chuckled and patted his cheek. 'One more day or two isn't going to make all that much difference. Besides, I've got to prepare my parents.'

He looked shocked. 'They know?'

'Yes.'

He made a little stifled groan and reddened but the high colour was difficult to notice in the darkness.

'In fact — my father went looking for you today down at Raanujarvï.'

He was surprised. Then he turned embarrassed again. 'In two days all this could happen? Helene, I'm surprised that you'd believe I'd run away.'

She tried to remember exactly when she'd begun to believe he'd done that and couldn't, although she knew that, being otherwise alone with her dilemma, she'd been prepared to believe almost anything which was unpleasant, but less about *him,* actually, than about *herself.*

She took his fingers and pulled. They walked round front of the log building and stopped to gaze up the moon-lighted roadway where small orange squares of light shone among the ugly, square, strictly functional log buildings of the village. She sighed.

'One more obstacle, Hans.'

'Your parents?'

'Well; my father at least.'

'Let me talk to him, Helene.'

'No. First I'll have to prepare the way. I'll do it in the morning at the store.' She turned, softly smiling. 'Just stay down here until I've had a chance to get him into an acceptable mood. Will you do that?'

'I'll do anything you ask. But there is this other thing — the actual business of getting married. I've never seen a minister in Joki.'

'We have one, Hans. We have a small church as well. But let's not plan too far ahead.'

He shrugged. 'I'll leave it in your hands. Only — don't put it off too long.' He swept a sidewards glance at her flat middle, then looked embarrassed again.

She wanted to throw herself into his arms one more time and let all the flood-gates of her powerful love overwhelm them again. Instead, keeping close rein on her emotions, she raised up, kissed him on the lips, dropped down and turned away.

He stood watching her walk away as he'd had other occasions to do, standing within the near-

shadows of the hostel tall and straight and handsome. He didn't know how *she* felt, but he could
analyse his own feelings easily: he was choked by
an emotion that seemed about to suffocate him.

Farther away the dog across from the
Vasaanen residence barked for the last time that
night as he picked up the hurrying sound of light
footfalls coming through the night where Helene
walked along.

CHAPTER TWENTY

'Bring Him To Me!'

Franz seemed half disinclined to go down to the store when Helene waited for him to get his hat. He grumbled something about it to Marta but all his wife did was push the hat at him and point towards the door where their daughter was waiting.

He said, 'The leg is troublesome.'

Marta sniffed. 'It wasn't troublesome when you went on your wild goose chase down to Raanujarvï so I suppose it'll manage to support you as far as the store.'

Passing his daughter and jerking on the hat, he said, 'Let that be a lesson to you, Helene; there is nothing more shrewish than a wife!'

Marta winked and Helene winked back.

As things turned out, once he was back where he should be, behind his counter and among his shelved goods, Franz Vasaanen forgot his ill humour. Customers came and went. Trygve Vesainen came by and Franz went to the cash drawer, took out some money and quietly passed it over. Trygve nodded and left. Franz looked sheepishly at his daughter.

'What I owed him for the ride yesterday,' he muttered and hastened forward scarcely limping when Gunnar Mainpaa came by for flour and sugar. He kept Gunnar in conversation for quite a while.

Helene reflected upon the nuances of human nature while awaiting the proper opportunity; right now her father was on the defensive over having taken money from the cash drawer to pay Trygve. But the moment she started speaking about what was uppermost in her mind *she* would be on the defensive and he no longer would be.

The clock said ten before the trade trickled off and they had a little while to replenish the shelves from the back-room storehouse. She helped, setting things up he brought forth, limping as he worked. She tried to devise a practical yet simple means of introducing Hans into their crisp conversation, but there was no way.

Franz said: 'Seven two-pound bags of flour.'

She said, 'Seven. That fills the shelf. Now tinned meat.'

How did one insinuate love and marriage between flour and tinned meat? One didn't. She waited until he went after more articles, leaned briefly atop the counter, saw people passing by on the road outside, decided there just was no persuasive way to mention what she had to discuss, and when he limped back, set the little carton of tins atop the counter and began fumbling inside to get the tins out, she said, 'Father; Hans and I are going to be married.'

He dropped a tin, ignored it, twisted and looked at her. She saw the shock her words had

produced and hastened on before he could interrupt.

'He didn't run away. He simply went down to
send a telegram to his parents about us. Last
night he showed me their reply. They are glad
for him. They only cautioned him to be very certain.'

'Last night? You mean to say he came to the
house last night?'

'Well; I met him — later, after supper.'

'Helene! You went out again at night and met
this — German!'

She sighed. The anger was up now, exactly as
she'd feared it would be. No one argued with her
father when he was angry. He wasn't reasonable
then. She leaned on the counter. This would
have to be the exception to the rule.

'I met him last night, Father, and I'm going to
meet him again. He asked me to marry him because —'

'Yes! Yes indeed! Because he is one of those
Germans who think being compromised is worse
than dishonour. I know the type — arrogant,
stiff, unbending —'

She flashed back at him, 'Stop always referring
to everyone you dislike as German. Father, I'm
in love with Hans. Very much in love with him.
He's very much in love with me. He's asked me
to marry him and I'm going to accept. In fact,
I've already accepted!'

'Do you realize what this will mean? He may
marry you because of the —'

'He didn't know — until after he'd asked me to marry him!'

'How is that? Of course he'd know.'

'Even if he had — he's still asked and I've still accepted.'

Franz stood, nostrils flaring, facing the daughter who also showed temper of her own for the first time that he could recall. Perhaps it was this grim and violent rebellion that kept him dumb for a long while.

He looked at the tinned meat under his hand, looked out into the warm sunlight, looked back at his daughter and said, controlling his voice with effort, 'Listen to me, Helene; the other way is better. This man will marry you, the child will have a name, then you will repent for as long as you live and the child will mature in the kind of environment that makes outcasts and criminals.'

She took a moment to lose some of her indignation. She reached over, took up several tins and turned away to arrange them on a shelf. She said nothing at all but her very silence emphasized the determination she'd evidenced moments earlier.

Franz watched for a while, then also turned grim and stubborn. It might have been comical if they both hadn't been so bitterly in opposition, for each time he'd hand her up several tins she would nod her head and accept them.

Later, just as they were finishing up, Gunnar Mainpaa strolled in wiping the back of his neck with a white handkerchief. He blew out a big breath and said he wished summer would go and winter would return.

Gunnar still had a patch of bandage on the side of his head but that didn't annoy him nearly as much as the free hand someone had employed in cutting away all the surrounding hair. It made him look odd enough and he knew it. But now he'd heard something else.

'Eric,' he told them, 'was buried down at Raanujarvï. That captain of the mountaineers called a little while ago. He asked me to tell you that Eric was buried in the black uniform and with the Iron Cross pinned on his front.'

Franz leaned upon the counter looking glum. It was noon but he had no appetite. Actually, he didn't care what had been done with Eric, but he listened politely and murmured a non-committal sentence.

'For him it is over. I have a hard time making up my mind about Eric. I'd just like to forget it. *All* of it.'

Mainpaa stood a moment in thought then quietly agreed, watched Helene take up several empty cartons and head for the storeroom with them, and said, 'The boy who was up there at Eric's cabin — he's camped down at the hostel again.'

Franz raised his eyes but said nothing. The silence between them became a little awkward so Gunnar left. When Helene returned Franz was putting on his hat. He mumbled about an errand and limped out into the golden daylight. She had one more empty carton to take away but as she reached for it atop the counter she saw her father turn southward.

As before, she speculated on the legitimate purposes he'd have for going away, but she was also very much aware of who else was down in that direction. Leaving the box on the counter she ran swiftly over to the door and watched.

Once, several of the villagers who'd been among the group who'd gone after the brigands, halted Franz and spoke for a few minutes with him. Then he got clear and resumed his way. She waited for him to enter one of the other business establishments but he kept right on limping along. Before he'd reached the last store she knew where he was going. She also knew Doctor Leino had the Luger so at least on that score Hans was safe, but her father was a burly, strong and determined man. She stepped forth and started in pursuit. Not that she feared for Hans; he was larger, just as physically powerful as her father, and many years younger. If there were blows she believed her father would come off second best, particularly in view of his bad leg. But she didn't want it to come to that, for if there was once a serious fight the chances of amicability resulting afterwards would be considerably minimized.

She dared not run; there were many people along both sides of the roadway, but Franz was too far ahead for her to catch him otherwise. Then came an intervention she was grateful for.

Kasimir Mainpaa stepped out into her father's path halting the older man. Kasimir spoke and Franz answered.

Helene walked as swiftly as she dared without attracting attention. It wasn't easy because several idling villagers called to her. She smiled back and kept right on walking. If only Kasimir could keep her father occupied a little longer!

He didn't; probably Kasimir would have been willing but her father was a resolute man and got out of more conversation some way and went deliberately limping along.

Now, there was no chance for her to intercede. She saw her father angle over into the shade near the doorway of the hostel. She also saw Kasimir's quizzical expression as she mechanically smiled at his greeting and hurried onward.

Franz went into the log building, which was cool and slightly shadowy because there were only two windows in the entire building, one set into the logs of each wall.

The place was empty.

He turned, limped back outside and walked around the north side which faced the village. There was nothing on that side of the place either. He turned and went round to the south side, which is where Helene caught up with him, breathless and anxious.

'If you want him I'll bring him to you,' she said, rushing the words together in her anxiety.

Franz turned, his eyes narrowed against sunlight, his jaw square-set and rock-hard. 'You won't have to bring him. I'll find him.'

'And if you do?'

He stood looking straight at her as uncompromising as a stone idol. She panted a little as she moved into the shade. 'Do you want everyone in the village to know, Father? Then stop acting this way.'

'Stop?'

'Please, Father. He is good and I love him. Isn't that what matters? You said you wanted to protect me; then act like you meant it.'

'Yes of course,' he said dourly. 'And let this — this — !'

'Boy,' she finished for him. 'Not "German", just this boy, or this man!'

'Where is he?'

'I don't know. I thought he was down here too.'

'No matter, Helene. I'll find him.'

'I hope you don't Father. Even without your injured leg you wouldn't be a match for him.'

'We'll see about that!'

She stepped over, caught his arm and made him turn towards her. He'd been about to go stalking back up through the village. 'Father; if you touch him — if you so much as lay a hand on Hans, I'll . . .'

'Yes? You'll do what, Helene?'

She sniffled and bit her lip to keep from crying. He blinked, looked at her face, watched as she withdrew the hand, then seemed to slump inside his clothing as though he were growing smaller even as he stood there. Finally, speaking roughly, he said, 'Helene; all right. You bring him to me.'

'No!'

'No? You've been begging me to see him. Now I'm saying I'll do that.' He looked at her again. 'Well; don't cry for heaven's sake, Helene. You're a nineteen-year-old woman. I never liked it when you cried. Now you go find this — this — all right then, this *young man* — and you bring him to me and your mother.'

'So you can make me wish I was dead, Father?'

Franz looked shocked. 'What are you talking about? What a thing to say!'

'You'll rage at him. You'll call him a German and every other unpleasant name you can think — !'

'*Be quiet!* Helene, don't you speak to me like this! I didn't say I'd be unpleasant to him. All I said was for you to bring him to the house where your mother and I will be waiting.'

Franz drew himself up, looked down his nose at his daughter, turned and went stamping back the way he'd come. As soon as he'd passed from shadow to sunlight Helene began to have a first glimmer of hope. She almost smiled through the tears; she recalled how it had been years back when she'd cried, and for all the intervening years she'd forgot entirely — her father'd never been able to stand up to her tears. Inadvertently she'd used the one tactic for which old Franz had no defence.

'Hello.'

She whirled. Hans was standing there, his hair wet, his face glistening. He'd been down the little path through the trees to the place where the over-turned fishing boats were beached, evidently bathing!

She stepped round the side of the building, threw herself into his arms and huddled there while he patted her shoulders and let her cry against his chest, more bewildered than ever.

CHAPTER TWENTY-ONE

Face To Face

After Franz had told his wife everything she stood at the stove saying over her shoulder, 'Well; it's now close to supper time and where are they?'

He was defensive. 'How would I know?' He fidgeted uneasily. 'Maybe it has taken her this long to find him.'

'Humph! I doubt that.' Marta looked around. 'Are you certain that's all you said to her, Franz; no ultimatums, no big threats?'

'Don't be ridiculous. Of course there were no ultimatums. Although for a moment she almost gave *me* an ultimatum.'

'She had reasons.'

Franz looked pained. 'Marta; I'm only trying to protect her. That's all I've ever wanted to do. And have done, as a matter of fact, up until the time this — *young man* — came along. Why couldn't he have taken one of the other roads on his tour? Joki isn't a very colourful village. He could have gone over by —'

'Well he didn't, Franz. Here; drink this coffee. Wait. Would you like some brandy in it?'

'Yes please. That would be very nice.' He took the cup and held it while she went rummaging for the bottle. 'Marta; we don't know this — *young man* — at all. How will he support a wife;

where will he get the money for the hospital and all the things he'll need afterwards for both his wife and son?'

Marta returned, poured brandy into the cup with a miser's squinted eye, then capped the bottle and went to put it away as she said, 'How did you, when there was nothing in Finland but foreign soldiers and hunger and devastation?'

He sipped, smacked his lips, went to a chair and eased down favouring his injured leg. 'That was different; we used military hospitals. What other kind were there?'

Marta brought the conversation back to the present. 'They'll make do exactly as we made do, Franz.'

'A German,' he muttered.

She turned that over in her mind because she too had matured during the German-hating period. 'Suppose he had been a Russian?' she asked.

Franz grimaced. 'What kind of a choice is that to ask someone to make? I'd take the Russian.'

'Do you know what your father would have said if he'd been standing here when you said that?'

'Marta; times change.'

'That's the point, Franz. *Times change.* This young man wasn't even born back during the war.'

'Well; perhaps his father was, or an uncle. They would have been —'

'You said I should stop being ridiculous!'

Franz finished the coffee, put the cup on the table and rolled a caustic eye round to his wife where she was back at work in front of the stove.

'Why do you always take everyone's part against me?'

She turned. 'Against you! Franz Vasaanen that's not true and you know it.'

'Lately it has been true and —'

'Lately you've acted like a partisan all over again. What of that foolishness rushing off into the forest after those brigands, with a wife and child and a business left behind?'

'Someone had to do it and the police wouldn't. You've said yourself a dozen times over the years someone should go after those Germans.' He blinked. 'Those brigands. I've heard you say that a hundred times.'

'Of course I said it. But I didn't mean *you*, a man past his prime.'

Franz's eyes flashed fire. 'Past my prime! I didn't even get tired until the second day. When the fighting started I was right up there with —'

'A hero,' grumbled Marta, turning her back on him. 'Franz; all right, you were a hero. But it wasn't for you to become, it was for the younger men and the soldiers. As for the rest of it — you were foolish to take the gun and go down to Raanujarvï. It's a wonder the entire village isn't laughing at you. Then today.'

'You weren't there.'

'I didn't have to be. I've lived with you a quarter of a century. You were angry with

Helene so I can imagine what you said.'

Franz turned on the chair with exaggerated patience. 'All I said was — bring the — *young man* — home so your mother and I can talk to him, can see him. That's all.'

'Then where are they?' demanded Marta, raising her head to peer out into the late evening shadows. 'Does it take this long to walk from the hostel to the north end of the village?'

'Well; how would I know where they are. And I don't like it either.' He looked longingly at the empty coffee cup. 'If she's going to marry him maybe it's all right.'

'It would be much better if they were already married.'

He decided to get another cup of coffee and reached for the cup. Marta turned, saw what he was about, got the pot and filled the cup he held out to her. But then she adamantly shook her head at his quizzical glance.

'No. No more brandy. Do you want to appear as a drunkard when they come?'

He sulked a little and asked when they could eat. Marta replied that they'd eat after Helene and her young man appeared. That, protested Franz, might not be for hours and his belly was making sounds of dissent now, not an hour from now.

Marta finally finished at the stove, got her own cup of coffee and sat at the kitchen table across from him. She smiled. It was a soft-sad little smile but at least it showed a change from her critical attitude of moments before.

'We should have had more children, Franz.'

He looked shocked, then thoughtful, and finally with a great sigh he muttered, 'Heaven forbid. If we'd had more girls — well — it would have put me in my grave. And boys — well — boys would have found him down at Raanujarvï and we'd all be in mourning now one way or the other. No; I think Helene has been quite enough.'

'They will go to Germany to live.'

He nodded, looked into the cup on the table and said, 'I can certainly think of better places to live. Still; Helene is young and very adaptable.'

'They will come to visit often, Franz, and bring the little girl.'

He looked up quickly. 'Little — what?'

Marta's smile vanished, her head stiffened on her shoulders, her eyes met his glance steadfastly. 'Little girl!'

He arose resolutely, went to the cupboard, got the brandy bottle, laced his coffee, tipped a few drops into her cup, put the bottle away and reseated himself before saying one more time: 'Heaven forbid!'

For ten seconds they sat in melancholy silence then the dog across the road began to furiously bark and Marta gulped the last of her coffee, arose, patted her hair into place, forgot she was wearing an apron and said, 'Franz; you be very careful what you say!'

Helene smiled at her mother across the

threshold. The tall, fair man with her also smiled, but with enquiry in each line of his expression. Marta stepped away for them to enter. Helene said, 'Mother, this is Hans Einhorst.'

Marta was extremely careful that her face should reveal nothing except courtesy. She saw at once the handsome young man was very uncomfortable and that made her feel less so as she led them to chairs in the parlour. Once, shooting a quick glance over a shoulder, she sought her husband in the kitchen doorway. He was not there. She knew a little sensation of annoyance. *Now* what was he up to?

'I have supper ready,' said Marta, and at the young man's forming dissent Marta raised a broad hand. 'Please; there is too much for just Helene's father and me.'

She turned and hustled to the kitchen in time to catch Franz hastily putting away the brandy bottle. Without a word Marta picked up his cup, flung the contents down the drain, caught his arm and gave him a fierce shove towards the doorway. She followed, smiling.

Hans arose when Franz limped into the room, his eyes bright, his face ruddy. Helene introduced them. They touched hands then sat and Marta, moving benignly across behind her husband's chair, gave him the sharp bone of her elbow in the back. He winced, cleared his throat and said, 'Would you like a little brandy before supper?' He was looking at the handsome young man making his private assessments.

Hans declined saying that he'd had a beer earlier in the afternoon and that was about his limit. Franz considered this; he'd known his share of Germans in previous times and he'd never known one before who considered one beer any kind of limit.

Marta picked up the lagging conversation although actually she was even worse at idle talk than her husband who'd at least had experience in *persiflage* at the store. But she had a time of it for the best of all reasons; she already knew of her daughter's intimacy with this handsome man and it embarrassed her no end just on that account to meet his gaze.

There was, however, one area where they could all converse with no peril. Marta chose it instinctively. 'We knew Eric Vendson since Helene was a child. A baby almost. It was very hard to believe that all this time he was hand-in-glove with those — brigands. Many an evening he's sat right there where you are sitting, Mister Einhorst, visiting, with neither of us suspecting for a moment he was other than we thought him.'

Hans nodded correctly. Evidently he was even less gifted at conversation under stress than either his host or hostess. Marta looked desperately at her daughter. She'd said all she could think of and unless they were now to all sit like lumps of clay gazing round, it was going to have to be Helene who prevented it.

She was ready. In a perfectly normal tone of

voice Helene said, 'Hans and I have been discussing our future.'

Both Franz and Marta sat a little straighter in their chairs.

'We think it would be best to be married here, then go down to Essen where he still has one year more at the University before he will graduate as an engineer.'

The ice was broken at last and if Hans didn't take a very large part in the ensuing conversation, both Helene's mother and father did. Franz said, 'Of course if that's what you think is best, but I was just wondering — hmmm — perhaps later on, possibly next spring, if you'd like your mother could go down and stay with you.'

Helene smiled softly at her father. 'We'd like that,' she said, and turned her head. 'Wouldn't we, Hans?'

He nodded. 'Very much.'

'And,' murmured Franz, considering his broad, scarred hands which lay in his lap, 'of course there will be a decent dowry.' He was careful to avoid Hans's eyes as he made this statement, which were fully upon him.

Marta made a little nervous laugh. 'Of course. People going to school have more expenses than other people — I think.'

Helene eased them all over this awkward moment by saying perhaps she'd better go see to the supper, and arose. At once her mother jumped up. They left the room together.

Hans smiled at Helene's father, who smiled

back. There was a wall-clock near the fireplace that did not ordinarily make a lot of noise. Now it did, sounding louder than ever in the uncomfortable silence until Franz forced himself to say, 'An engineer, eh? That's an honourable profession. Tell me — young man — when you graduate will you then be entitled to survey forests?'

Hans flushed. 'No sir; I'll be a different kind of an engineer.'

'Of course,' murmured Franz, whose knowledge of engineers and engineering was sketchy. 'Well; but it is still a good profession.' He said this heartily enough but the look on his face seemed to leave room for doubt. 'And your father — he is also an engineer?'

'No sir. My father operates a steel mill.'

'Ahhh?' murmured Franz, eyebrows slowly climbing. 'A foreman?'

'No sir. He owns it. That is, he owns most of the stock and is President of the Board of Directors.'

Franz was awed. He'd seen steel mills once or twice in his lifetime; they were great, noisy complexes of railroad sidings, noise, smoke, people and formidable confusion. He was enormously impressed by Hans's words. In fact he began to think back to his own highest expectations for his daughter — with luck she might have married a policeman or a professional man; perhaps even one of the summer tourists from possibly England or America. He had never in his wildest imaginings considered it possible for Helene to marry the son of a great industrialist.

Marta and Helene appeared in the kitchen doorway. Supper was ready. Franz arose, winced, adjusted his heft to the unimpaired leg and swept a wide gesture towards his soon-to-be-son-in-law. 'You first, Hans my boy.'

CHAPTER TWENTY-TWO

A Three-Quarter Moon

For Hans it was an escape when he and Helene finally left the house. Not that he hadn't found her parents solid folk, but as he explained while they strolled through the soft-balmy late summer evening, he'd never been adept at casual conversation until he got to know the other people, and it seemed that her parents suffered from some similar affliction.

She took his arm, hugged it close and smiled upwards. 'You did very well. Even my father seemed to like you.' She sighed quietly thinking it had been quite a change in her father from hours earlier. 'If you really don't think very much of my mother coming to visit us when the baby is born . . .'

'Of course she should come,' he said quickly. 'That's how things should be.'

The village was quiet, as always at night, with its small squares of cheery light at the windows they passed. He watched the way she looked round and said it would probably be sad for her to leave Joki. She only partially agreed.

'I was born here, grew up here, know all the people, the places to go in summertime, the slopes to ski upon, the ponds for skating in wintertime. But no, I don't expect to miss it the way

213

you mean. Not with homesickness, but always with very fond memories.' She looked up at him. 'Anyway, it won't have disappeared. We could come back some day, if you wanted to.'

He nodded. They would come back of course. When their child was old enough and sturdy enough to perhaps swim in the estuary or ski the lower hills or tramp the forest.

He said, 'Helene; there is something I've purposefully never told you.'

She almost stopped but he kept hold of her and walked on. She felt fear in her breast but smiled bravely and said, 'That you already have a wife.'

'No. It's about my parents.'

'They won't like me?'

'They'll love you. My mother especially because she said I was supposed to have been a daughter. No; it's simply that they are wealthy.'

She digested that. 'Oh. Well; perhaps if we work hard enough at it we can overcome that, Hans.'

He looked at her sharply but she was elfishly grinning so he sighed. 'You know how it is nowadays; everyone thinks people who have money must have got it by squeezing sweat from less fortunate people.' He looked at her again, soberly. 'We've never discussed politics — things like that.'

'Should we have, Hans?'

'Well; if you are one of those activist girls . . .'

She'd read enough newspapers to know what

an activist was but that was the extent of her knowledge in that direction so she said, a trifle naïvely, 'Is Germany a place where people talk politics and internationalism all the time?'

It was his turn to smile. 'No; but there is more feeling for it there. Here, the villagers seem less involved; their lives are simple and orderly — except when brigands appear of course. But in Essen — well — there's more awareness of the world on all sides. There has to be; Germany is an industrial state.'

She shrugged slightly and was conscious of the brush of their arms, shoulders, thighs, as they reached her father's store and moved slowly past. 'I'll have my hands full enough with other things, Hans. I'm sure of that. Anyway, politics never interested me very much. I'm what Germans might call an inherent *hausfrau*.'

He was relieved. He also asked if she knew more German words because if she didn't they were going to have a truly international homelife; she being Finnish, he German, neither fluent in the language of the other so conversing in English.

Her only comment was a dispassionate: 'Would it matter?'

'Not in the least,' he assured her.

'And of course I'll learn German in time. Although it's never sounded very pretty to me.'

He laughed. 'It's not the sounds of a language that make it pretty, love, it's the words used.'

'Very wisely said, Hans.'

A crooked shadow loomed ahead. Someone was balancing near their side of the road as though to step down and cross to the far side. She recognized the shadow at once.

'Kasimir Mainpaa.'

He nodded, watching the cripple. 'The evening they came to accuse me of making you cry, this one was the only man who held back.'

Kasimir saw them and continued to hesitate. He smiled as they came up and halted. 'Wonderful evening,' he said by way of greeting, and didn't miss the way she was hugging Hans's arm to her as they stood close together under the three-quarter moon. 'But I can smell autumn too, which is as it must be. Summers always end, eh?'

She recalled her last conversation with the cripple down near the estuary where the boats were turned wrong-side-up. It made her slowly see Kasimir as different from how she'd viewed him before. Very quietly she said, 'A summer will end, yes, but other things just begin.'

Kasimir's eyes considered her expression as he nodded. Whether Hans understood or not, she and Kasimir did. 'Good things,' he replied, and extended his hand to Hans.

They shook and Kasimir threw them a wide smile tinged with a light edging of sadness, then turned and scuttled on across the road towards his house. Hans gazed after him.

'Deeper than he looks, Helene. That one is a lot more man inside than he is outside.'

They walked almost to the hostel then she paused to turn for a look back up through the village. It had always looked about as it now appeared in the moonlight, except of course during the harsh winters, then it looked even more fairyland-like with its rounded white roofs and deep-rutted road, its mounds of white-drift, its straight-standing fragrant woodsmoke. Hans had been right; she would miss it.

He led her into the shadows by one hand and placed his sleeping bag against the log building so she'd have a decent place to sit.

'It's still hard to believe,' he told her, watching moonlight filter down through the high limbs of that trimmed tree and softly mantle her face, throat and shoulders. 'Just a brief tour through Scandinavia — and I didn't even complete it. Didn't even get very well started in fact, before — you — happened to me.'

She thought that wasn't all that had happened to him but all she said was, 'I want you to be very certain, Hans.'

He nodded. 'I wish I could have been as certain of everything in my life as I am of this.' He grinned. 'But I'll admit it was like a bolt from the blue; I had no idea a man could simply see a girl and feel everything he'd ever thought about girls before just simply drop away.'

She wasn't sure just what he meant by that but caution suggested that she'd better not try to find out. 'About the wedding,' she said, and added nothing to it.

'I told you, Helene; it's in your hands.'

'There couldn't be a very large wedding anyway, Hans. Neither the village nor the church are up to that. Perhaps friends, neighbours, relatives. . . . Your parents?'

He said he'd hire Trygve Vesainen to drive him down to Raanujarvï in the morning so he could telegraph an invitation, but then he also said he wasn't sure his father would even be in Germany because he travelled all over the world. In order to keep her from feeling uneasy about the improbability of his parents making it, he said it would be nice if they were there for the ceremony but it wasn't strictly necessary.

She nodded, half hearing, half dreaming. There were a lot of things neither of them had mentioned and of course there were hundreds of explanations which would have to be given as time progressed. She wondered if their both coming from different environments was going to make it difficult for them. She even said something about that, hesitantly.

He brushed it aside. 'We can't speak each other's language but we found a way to communicate didn't we?'

She was warmed by his staunchness but when she arose and he came up too, reaching, she turned cautious again. They kissed, she pushed clear and touched his face with one cool hand.

'I'll see the minister tomorrow, Hans. I'll see about the church too.'

'You'll need money,' he said and plunged a

hand into a trouser pocket.

She shook her head at him. 'Not now. Not to-night. Wait until daytime for that.'

He looked a little perplexed until she tipped her face to the three-quarter moon and the much closer treetop above them, then he understood. This wasn't the time to speak of money.

'Come to the house tomorrow night, Hans. For dinner. Please?'

He promised. He also said her mother was a wonderful cook and that since leaving Essen he hadn't actually tasted a home-cooked meal.

He would have walked her home but she declined the offer and after one more light kiss, went off by herself. Once, she turned. He waved from the doorway of the hostel.

She was in no greater hurry to return home than she'd been to reach the hostel where she'd left him. It was an exquisite night. Actually it was no different from any other late summer night except that perhaps there was a little more moonlight than usual. But she detected the scents of spruce and pine and balsam with more clarity. She saw each star as an individual blue-white entity instead of part of some hazy, crowded galaxy. She saw the village in gentler perspective too and paused a moment before the locked door of her father's shop. Reaching, she could touch the worn old latch.

Then she moved on past all the little fences, past a few darkened houses, for although it was not very late, a good many villagers habitually retired early. The dog across from her own home didn't hear her until she was almost out front of her parents' home, then he must have been tired because he did little more than emit one healthy bark, then growl a little.

Her parents were waiting up. They watched her enter. Marta was a little wet-eyed but she smiled bravely. Helene thought of their part in all this and her heart expanded towards them for the suffering, the anguish, the terrible uncertainty she'd brought them.

Her father had his impaired leg propped upon a low ottoman as he smiled upwards. 'Well; it is a very pleasant night out, eh?'

She went over, put both arms round his thick neck and squeezed. 'It is the most beautiful night out I've ever seen. It might even be the most beautiful night of all time.'

Marta considered her knitting in a little bag of carpeting beside her chair but didn't take it up. 'Did you know Hans's parents are very wealthy?' she asked Helene.

The answer was simple. 'No, Mother; not until he told me a little while ago. But it wouldn't have mattered what they were because I'm marrying Hans, not his parents.'

'Well; when you are married though, you'll have to mind your manners in Essen. You must always be a pride to your husband, Helene. A genuine credit to him.'

'Yes Mother.'

'And the children must obey their father. You

see, that's how the Germans raise their young. Not like us — too much liberty and leniency.'

Helene watched her mother's face as the older woman spoke. It was a strong, logical, fair face, toughened by many adversities but by no means made hard nor unrelenting. She thought it must have been very difficult in her mother's time for a woman. Very hard.

'. . . And since Hans is such a handsome man, Helene, you must always keep yourself neat and pretty. Even when there is no one around.'

Franz looked at his daughter and slowly, surreptitiously winked. But he did not interrupt his wife. In fact he had nothing at all to say until she was finished, or at least had to re-group her thoughts before launching into another sermon.

'Have you discussed the ceremony?' he inquired.

'Here in Joki, Father, at the church, with a few friends, perhaps some neighbours; nothing elaborate because it isn't necessary. Hans is going down to Raanujarvï in the morning to telegraph his parents an invitation. He doesn't think his father will be able to make it.'

'Well then I'll be father to both of you,' said Franz, and smiled broadly, his breath tinged with the aromatic scent of brandy.

Marta arose and hugged her daughter, then turned and went into the bedroom. Franz, looking after her, also arose. He kissed Helene on both cheeks, gripped her fingers, then smiled as she turned to climb the stairs. When she was no longer in sight Franz sighed, went round switching off the lights, and finally went in where his wife was already under the blankets gazing at the ceiling.

'You were brave,' he told her, stopping to pat a work-roughened hand. 'I know. People may not think a father knows how a thing like this affects a mother, but I know. But he is a fine lad.'

'Come to bed,' said Marta, dabbing at her eyes with a balled up handkerchief.

Franz nodded and said no more. He was melancholy as he worked out of his shoes and socks and shirt. Life has an inexorable pattern. No matter how a man would hope to hold it back just for a little longer, he never can do so. Well; then of course the next best thing to do is grow old gracefully.

He got into the huge old bed, pulled covers under his chin and patted Marta's hand again. This time she patted him back.